"It's a masquerade party. The point is to conceal one's identity."

Jayden couldn't help the smile tugging at the corners of his mouth. Whoever she was underneath that mask, she had a quick mind and a sharp tongue. Two characteristics he suddenly decided were his absolute favorites in a woman.

"Don't be that way, darlin'. How are we ever going to get to know each other if you don't tell me who you are?"

She looked away briefly before bringing her gaze back to his. When she did, there was a twinkle of something mischievous in it that made his heart race and his blood run hot.

"But if I told you, I'd miss out on the fun of watching you try to figure out who I am. I'm not sure I can willingly give that up just to satisfy your curiosity."

"Trust me, my queen. My curiosity isn't what I want satisfied."

* * *

Cinderella Masquerade by LaQuette is part of the Texas Cattleman's Club: Ranchers and Rivals series.

Dear Reader,

Welcome to my first rodeo in Royal in the Texas Cattleman's Club continuity, *Cinderella Masquerade*.

In this fairy-tale retelling, we meet Dr. Zanai James, a reserved, sweet soul who would rather get lost in her beloved science books than deal with people. Science makes sense, people don't. Which is why she has no intention of attending the annual masquerade ball at the TCC. Unfortunately for Zanai, she has a pushy best friend who knows her way around a costume. Before Zanai can break in her glass slippers, she's at the ball, catching the eye of Royal's very own Prince Charming. Although flirting is a foreign concept to her, she's emboldened by her concealed identity and indulges in the fantasy and temptation of Jayden Lattimore.

Too afraid she'll turn back into a pumpkin when the clock strikes twelve, Zanai steals away into the night before Jayden can discover her identity or satisfy the mutual desire between them. Frustrated that the temptress in red slipped through his fingers, Jayden vows to uncover who his mystery red queen is underneath the mask. A diamond-and-ruby earring and the heated memory of her in his arms are the only clues he has. It may not be much, but Jayden will comb through all of Royal to find the only woman who makes his blood burn and his nature rise.

Keep it sexy!

LaQuette

LaQUETTE

CINDERELLA MASQUERADE

HARLEQUIN
DESIRE

Special thanks and acknowledgment are given to LaQuette for her contribution to the Texas Cattleman's Club: Ranchers and Rivals miniseries.

Recycling programs for this product may not exist in your area.

ISBN-13: 978-1-335-58145-7

Cinderella Masquerade

Harlequin Enterprises ULC
22 Adelaide St. West, 41st Floor
Toronto, Ontario M5H 4E3, Canada
www.Harlequin.com

Printed in U.S.A.

A 2021 Vivian Award finalist and DEIA activist in the romance industry, **LaQuette** writes sexy, stylish and sensational romance. She crafts dramatic, emotionally epic tales that are deeply pigmented by reality's paintbrush.

This Brooklyn native writes unapologetically bold, character-driven stories. Her novels feature diverse ensemble casts who are confident in their right to appear on the page.

Books by LaQuette

Devereaux Inc.

A Very Intimate Takeover
Backstage Benefits
One Night Expectations

Texas Cattleman's Club

Cinderella Masquerade

Visit her Author Profile page at Harlequin.com or www.laquette.com for more titles.

You can also find LaQuette on Facebook, along with other Harlequin Desire authors, at www.Facebook.com/harlequindesireauthors!

To my only princess, Mackenzie.
You're the jewel of your auntie's eye.

One

"Absolutely not!" Zanai James shook her head and crossed her arms as she stared down her best friend in the whole world, Morgan Grandin. Considering the smile spreading on her friend's lips, Zanai was doubtful Morgan was taking her objection seriously. She never did.

"Come on, Zanai," Morgan fake whined as she stepped from behind the counter of her boutique, The Rancher's Daughter, and stepped in front of Zanai. "This is the party of the year. Anyone who is anyone attends. People start ordering their costumes nearly a year in advance to make sure they're prepared for the masquerade ball. You've spent years dodging this event, it's time for you to stop hiding."

Self-conscious about the truth her friend was hurling at her, Zanai looked down at the top of her very sensible Mary Jane–styled shoes.

"Morgan, I appreciate what you're trying to do. But it won't work. I don't fit in to spaces like these. Books, science, research, those things all make sense to me. Small talk and flirting are foreign concepts. Hell, I can't even bat my eyelashes properly. I look like I'm having some sort of seizure when I do."

"Zanai," Morgan huffed as she placed her hands on Zanai's shoulders. "You're beautiful and smart. People will love you if you just give them the chance to."

Zanai shook her head. "People find me awkward and boring."

"Hey, don't talk about my best friend like that. You're neither."

Zanai smiled at Morgan, loving how protective she was. "I didn't say I *was* awkward and boring. I said people *find me* to be so."

When Morgan's lifted eyebrow revealed she didn't get the distinction, Zanai continued. "Morgan, that wasn't a self-deprecating comment. I like the fact that I'm a nerd. I wear that badge proudly. It's just I'm smart enough to know other people don't appreciate that quality in me. So I stay away from them and live my best STEM life."

Morgan gave her a sad smile. Zanai knew her friend didn't pity her. Morgan just didn't think it was healthy for anyone to spend so much time alone.

"Zanai, you promised your aunt you wouldn't let your light be snuffed out by work and that pack of wolves masquerading as your family."

Guilt and grief tugged at the edges of Zanai's heart at the mention of the only loving influence she'd had in her life since her mother died when she was a child. Her mother's sister Déjà was everything bright and beautiful in Zanai's bleak little life. Losing her earlier in the year still weighed so heavily on her that she wondered if she'd ever truly recover from the loss.

"That's a low blow, using my dead aunt to manipulate me. I see now why you and Ryan fight so much. You don't let anything go."

"Encourage, not manipulate," Morgan corrected. "And Ryan is hardly a paragon of virtue. He's a thickheaded neanderthal that I'd sooner…"

Zanai couldn't hide the devilish grin blooming on her face. Morgan wasn't the only one in the room who knew how to get a reaction out of her best friend.

Morgan was usually sunshine and rainbows hopped up on sugar on most days. However, the mere mention of Ryan Carter's name and Morgan lost all her chill. Though her friend would never admit it,

Zanai suspected Morgan's dislike of the man had more to do with mutual attraction than anything else.

"We are not talking about Ryan or how infuriating he is. We're talking about how wonderful you are and how you need to live a little."

"I know." She huffed and walked over to a nearby settee in the fitting area. "I just don't know how to be at these things. I don't fit in. While other girls were figuring out how to be sociable proper ladies, my nose was stuck in a book. I don't know how to act or dress for these kinds of events. I'd be so out of place."

Morgan sat down next to her, wrapping a protective, comforting arm around her shoulders. "Your nose being stuck in a book helped you become a stellar developmental psychologist for neurodivergent kids. The good news is you're rich enough that you can pay for someone to do your hair and makeup. Also, your best friend in the whole world owns a boutique shop and has connections in the rag industry that also includes clothing fit for a queen. So, if you promise to let me have my wicked way with you, I'll make sure you're the prettiest girl at the ball."

Zanai looked at her friend with a skeptical glare. Morgan had that same determined look in her eye that always seemed to be there when she was about to do something that would probably land Zanai in the middle of something she'd more than likely want to shake Morgan for later.

Zanai closed her eyes and gathered just enough

strength to tell her friend no when her gaze landed on Morgan's face practically glowing with excitement. Like always, she could never deny Morgan anything when it made her eyes light up like the star on a Christmas tree.

"Fine, Morgan. Do your worst."

Three days later, Zanai stood in front of a mirror in Morgan's closed shop in absolute awe of her reflection.

"Morgan, how on earth did you pull this off in only a few days?"

The satisfied gleam in Morgan's eyes revealed the obvious pride she had in her creation.

"I told you I'd make you the prettiest girl at the ball."

Zanai stared at herself in front of the mirrored wall, barely recognizing the reflection shining back at her.

Her dress was a strapless ball gown with a scoop neckline bodice that accented her shapely torso and cinched her waist. The floor-length skirt was made of layers of chiffon falling into perfect folds. The dress was gorgeous, but the bright red color is what took Zanai's breath away.

"Morgan, I don't recognize myself."

Her friend clapped beside her as she let out an excited squeal.

"It's a masquerade ball, silly. You're not supposed

to recognize yourself. Let me get your accessories and we'll be ready to leave."

Morgan handed her a small silver clutch then draped the matching cape over Zanai's shoulders. Although the cape was made of a single layer of sheer chiffon, it made Zanai feel less exposed. Once again, her friend knew just what she needed.

Morgan swept Zanai's long dark curls over one shoulder before securing a sparkling crown on her head then sliding a red masquerade mask onto her face.

Zanai had to admit, she was stunning. She definitely looked like she belonged at the ball. Now, all she had to do was keep her mouth shut, and maybe folks at the Texas Cattleman's Club wouldn't recognize what an outsider she truly was.

Jayden Lattimore sipped his glass of champagne as he leaned on the bar looking out at the sea of people in the large ballroom. As always, it looked as if most of the elite in Royal had shown up for this annual ball.

Even with some portions of their faces being covered with a mask, Jayden could make out almost everyone milling around the room. With boredom clawing at him, he looked around to see if there was anything for him to get into before he made his exit.

Coming from one of the wealthiest families in Royal, he'd fulfilled his duty by showing up. But he wasn't about to spend his entire night bored to death at this excuse for grown rich folks to play dress up.

He was about to take another sip from his glass when a vision filled his gaze. A queen dripping in red stood at the entryway. He couldn't tell if she was purposely pausing for dramatic effect, or if she was just getting her bearings as she entered the room. Either way, more than a few heads turned to take in the elegant, yet sexy monarch gracing the rest of them with her presence.

Jayden was about to make his way over to where she stood when she stepped inside of the room and headed in his direction.

That suited him just fine. Usually, he was too easygoing to chase a woman. The truth was, coming from old money while standing at more than six feet with good looks meant he didn't have to chase anyone. Women came to him, not the other way around.

But even though she was literally approaching him, there was something about her air of mystery that intrigued Jayden enough that his interest in talking to her went beyond the usual cursory notice he had in the women he encountered.

"At the risk of sounding cliché, may I get you a drink?"

The masked queen glanced up at him with sultry deep brown eyes, and something akin to a sledgehammer slapped him in the center of his chest, forcing him to fight against the urge to take in a gasping breath.

"No, thank you." She answered quickly as she leaned into the bar and looked around the room. "I'm waiting for someone."

Disappointment flooded him. It would figure this alluring creature was attached.

"My friend needed to speak to someone out in the hall. She's going to meet me here shortly."

Jayden could feel a smile burgeoning on his face. She was here with her friend. Well, that changed everything, didn't it?

"Seems your friend's delay is my good fortune. Spending a few moments in the presence of the loveliest woman at the ball is no hardship at all."

He waited for the practiced dip in her head, the expected response ingrained in most of the women from the upper class of Royal. Feigned humility was something that was taught from the cradle. But not this woman. She stared at him openly as if she were trying to figure out what was going on in his head.

"Thank you for the compliment. But half my face is covered in a mask, how on earth can you tell if I'm beautiful or not?"

Her question was so blunt it amused him. She was definitely not using the normal script for an encounter like this.

"Wow," he laughed before taking a sip from his glass. "You don't hold back, do you?"

She blinked, then tucked an errant strand of hair behind an ear, making the ruby and diamond earrings dangling from her ears sway back and forth. When she tipped her head to the side and looked up at him, her eyes softened to a warm brown. "I'm sorry. I didn't mean to offend you. Small talk just isn't my strong suit."

He waved a dismissive hand. "No apologies necessary. It's actually quite refreshing to have a woman speak her mind to me. It levels the playing field if I know what she's thinking." He extended his hand, hoping against hope she would accept it. When she did, a spark of something unrecognizable but potent burned through his palm spreading like wildfire through his system.

"I'm Jayden Lattimore." He pointed a finger from the hand still holding his glass. "Otherwise known as the Phantom."

"I kind of figured that from the white mask that covers half your face."

He shrugged. "Well, when you've been to enough of these, you eventually run out of interesting costumes. A classic is easy to put together yet acceptable in these rarefied circles."

He didn't let go of her hand and he wasn't ignorant to the fact that she hadn't taken hers away.

"And you are?"

She formed her lips into the perfect O that made him contemplate how much he'd love to see her sultry mouth take that shape under an entirely different set of circumstances.

"It's a masquerade party, the point is to conceal one's identity."

Jayden couldn't help the smile tugging at the corners of his mouth. Whoever she was underneath that mask, she had a quick mind and a sharp tongue. Two characteristics he suddenly decided were his absolute favorite in a woman.

"Don't be that way, darlin'. How are we ever going to get to know each other if you don't tell me who you are? I'm at this party every year and I can tell you I've never seen you here or at the Texas Cattleman's Club, period. So, forgive me for being so taken by your breathtaking beauty that I'm clamoring to know your name."

She looked away briefly before bringing her gaze back to his. When she did, there was a twinkle of something mischievous in it that made his heart race and his blood run hot.

"But if I told you, I'd miss out on the fun of watching you try to figure out who I am. I'm not sure I can willingly give that up just to satisfy your curiosity."

"Trust me, my queen. My curiosity isn't what I want satisfied."

He waited a beat to see if his words offended her. He wasn't trying to be a smart-ass. Well, okay, he was definitely trying to be a smart-ass, but he wasn't attempting to offend her. Any worry he had about disrespecting her slipped away when her smile broadened.

"Seriously," he continued. "I'd love to find out who that lovely mask is concealing."

"Why?"

He narrowed his gaze as he contemplated his answer to her question. She was gorgeous in all that red. The way the fitted bodice clung to and lifted her small breasts definitely played a role in him wanting to know her better. But it was more than that. The way she looked at him, he could tell she wasn't the average socialite that attended these sorts of parties. There was something deeper and brighter shining through that drew him in.

"I want to know who you are because I want to know what to call you when we leave here and spend a little time together."

"Presumptuous, aren't you?"

He shrugged. "Confident. You've been here for a few minutes and you haven't attempted to get away from me yet. If I was getting on your nerves, something tells me you'd have found a way to shut me down by now. Besides that, I don't chase women. If a woman tells me she's not interested, I move on to the next. If you're not interested, all you have to do is say so."

There, he'd thrown down the gauntlet, placing the ball firmly in her court. Whatever happened next would be her decision, and more than anything he hoped her desires were aligned with his.

"There you are." Jayden's attention was pulled away by the intrusion. He felt the red queen's hand slip from his, leaving him with a strange sense of loss he couldn't understand.

He shook his head before looking at the woman interrupting them. Even with her face covered by a lace half mask and her red hair covered by a white-blond wig, he could recognize Morgan Grandin no matter her disguise. She was his best friend's sister and they'd spent enough time together as kids that he could pick her out of a crowd anywhere.

He glanced over Morgan's shoulder and saw Vic following closely behind.

"Two of the Grandin siblings, as always, your timing is perfect." Jayden hoped his words sounded as sarcastic as he'd meant them to.

"Jayden, can I speak to you for a minute?"

Apparently, Vic hadn't picked up on the bite he'd intended his greeting to have.

"I'm kind of in the middle of something, Vic. We can meet up later."

His friend placed a hand on his shoulder, pulling his attention from his red queen in front of him.

"This is important, Jay. It'll only take a few minutes."

Jayden cut sharp eyes at Vic before returning his gaze in the red queen's direction. Unfortunately, by the time he did, his mystery woman was quickly walking away with Morgan.

"Thanks for the cockblock, my friend."

"In that outfit, you'll easily locate her once I'm done talking." When Jayden groaned, Victor held up a hand to quiet him. "Just hear me out so you can get back to your mystery lady and I can get back to Aubrey."

At the mention of Vic's fiancée's name, Jayden could see the bright spark of joy flooding the man's gaze. Who could be mad at him when he looked that damn happy?

"Speak your piece so I can get back to what I was doing before you so rudely interrupted me."

"Someone's in a pissy mood." Vic raised a brow as he watched Jayden carefully.

A strip of red caught his eye and he quickly turned to see if it was the intriguing woman who'd held his attention, who was still holding his attention even now.

It wasn't her, and that realization brought him more disappointment than it should have. Considering they hadn't spent more than five minutes in each other's presence, he truly shouldn't care. Apparently his brain hadn't gotten the memo, though, because here he was trying to look around Vic to see if he could get her in his sights.

"I can see your focus is elsewhere." When Jayden didn't answer, Vic smiled because he'd known Jayden so long, he didn't need a verbal response to know what was going on in Jayden's head.

"I can see why you're so taken, but I really need you to bring it in. I need your help."

"With what?"

"I think I've figured out a way to get Ryan and Morgan together."

"Ryan and Morgan? Really?"

Ryan was a good friend of Jayden's. Although he knew Ryan was a decent man, he had really strong opinions and an authoritarian personality. Jayden wasn't completely convinced pairing him with Morgan, a woman who walked her own path despite what anyone else thought, was the best idea Victor had ever come up with.

"Come on, Jayden, it's obvious the two of them are seriously into each other. And if my sister is going to be with anyone, I'd rather it be a man I know actually cares about her."

Jayden agreed. He loved Morgan like a sister and Ryan was his friend. And although Jayden knew Vic wanted what was best for his sister, he had his suspicions about his motives.

"He does care about her, but I feel like your motivation is also grounded in the fact that you're so deliriously happy with Aubrey you're trying to match up everyone around you."

Vic didn't outright deny Jayden's claim, he just continued on as if Jayden hadn't said anything.

"They fight like alley cats." Vic's observation was an accurate one. Morgan and Ryan couldn't be in each other's presence more than two seconds before they started arguing about something. It was oddly entertaining, yet somewhat exhausting, to watch. "I'm just tired of their bickering. Besides, what's wrong with wanting the people around me to be as happy as I am?"

"Nothing," Jayden replied. "Just keep your busy-body matchmaking focused on your sister and leave my love life alone. I have no intention of being the next one on your list."

Having laid down the law, Jayden huffed loudly hoping to move this conversation along so he could find his red queen.

"What do you want to do, Vic?"

"I'm gonna send Morgan a message she'll assume was meant for Ryan. When she texts back, I'll tell her to disregard the message, it wasn't meant for her. She'll never be able to resist coming back over to try to force an explanation out of me. She'll no doubt come back over here to make me clarify my meaning. When she's within earshot, we let her overhear us talking about how much Ryan is into her."

Jayden tapped his finger against his champagne glass before speaking. "You really think that'll work?"

"It will work." Vic didn't give Jayden a chance

to respond before he was pulling his phone from his pocket and tapping out a quick text.

Jayden glanced over Vic's shoulder, watching Morgan make her way back to the bar sans the red queen. He noted his disappointment at the stranger's absence and sighed.

He could pretend it was just his curiosity that allowed him to care this much about the mystery woman's absence, but he knew it wasn't. There was something in the depths of her dark eyes that had taken hold of Jayden. And he knew he wouldn't be satisfied until he was able to explore it.

"All right, man. She's almost in position," Jayden noted quickly. "Let's get this done so I can get on with my evening."

"And back to that exquisite woman in red?"

His friend's penchant for being a pain in the ass was beginning to grate on Jayden's nerves.

"Do you want my help or not?"

Vic threw up his hands in surrender. Satisfied the subject had been dropped, Jayden swallowed the last of his champagne in one gulp.

"Good. Let's get this over with before Aubrey comes looking for you."

Vic waited until Morgan was safely within earshot before he began.

"It's such a shame that Ryan would never admit his true feelings to Morgan. It's obvious he's into her, and if she was actually paying attention, she would realize it too."

"Attraction that powerful can be hard to admit." Jayden saw Morgan stop from the corner of his eye. His words had definitely caught her attention. "Especially if you're afraid the other person will reject you."

Vic gave Jayden a knowing nod before continuing. "You're right. But they're both going to end up miserable for no reason at all. It's such a waste."

"You can't force people to do what's in their own best interest, Vic. Ryan and Morgan will either figure this out, or they won't. There's nothing you or anyone else can do about it."

Morgan stopped before turning on her heel and heading back in the direction she'd come. When she was far enough away, Vic smiled, happy his plan appeared to be working.

"I'm glad you're pleased. Now get out of my way so I can get back to what I was doing before you rudely interrupted me."

Jayden's body was thrumming with the anticipation of finding his mystery woman in red.

"Don't worry, friend. We're almost there. We just gotta do one more thing to get this plan underway."

Jayden sat his empty glass on the bar top then narrowed his gaze at his friend.

"What more do you want from me?"

"We gotta go find Ryan and tell him the same thing."

"I feel like we're back in elementary school passing notes between these two in class. All that's missing is the 'check yes if you like Ryan' box."

"Don't be so cynical, Jayden. Love is in the air. We're just helping it along."

Two

"And you're sure about this?"

Jayden kept his mouth shut, leaving opportunity for Vic to answer Ryan. This was his plan after all. Jayden saw no reason his friend shouldn't do the heavy lifting in this little scheme.

"Ryan," Vic continued, "no one knows my sister like me. All that annoyance is just frustration. She's really into you. She just doesn't think the feeling is mutual, so she lashes out."

From the corner of his eye, Jayden saw a flash of bright red. He turned to see his red beauty walking in the opposite direction.

"Hey, y'all. Excuse me for a moment. I've got something to take care of."

He didn't know whether his friends had agreed or not. Almost as soon as he'd spoken, his long legs were carrying him in the red queen's direction, eating up the distance between them.

"There you are. I finally found you." His words made her stop, pausing briefly before she turned around to face him.

"Found me? I wasn't aware I was lost."

"You were to me." That comment bought him a sincere smile that warmed him from the inside out, compelling him to step closer into her personal space.

"Dance with me, darlin'."

She watched for a moment, her silence stretching out so long he worried that she might actually deny his request. But at the last possible moment, she extended her hand to him and he clasped it in a gentle but firm grasp before pulling her into his embrace.

The music was slow as they swayed back and forth pressed so tightly together there was no clear line where she ended and he began.

"You still haven't told me your name. Who are you under that mask, my dear queen?"

"A little intrigue is good for the soul."

He chuckled at her response. "I'm almost certain that's not how that saying actually goes."

Her nonchalant shrug kept their banter going.

"That doesn't mean it's not true. The beauty of this night is we can be anything we want to be. So, it doesn't matter who I really am. It only matters who I want to be in this moment."

He looked down into her gaze, feeling a little buzzed. He hadn't consumed nearly enough alcohol to feel any of its effects. The only thing he could attribute it to was the alluring woman in his arms.

"And who do you want to be in this moment, m'lady?"

She smiled again, drawing him closer into her web. He could feel her luring him in, but could do nothing to stop it. The truth was, he didn't want to.

"The woman dancing with you."

He was careful as he tightened the circle of his arms, like he was touching something breakable. It wasn't that he thought her too delicate for his touch. The gleam of need and burning desire flashing in her eyes revealed everything he needed to know about how much she could handle.

No, this wasn't about her being too fragile. It was about fear. His fear to be precise. He was afraid that if he was too abrupt, it would shatter the moment, the cocoon they'd made for themselves in the middle of the dance floor. They were surrounded by other bodies, but somehow, it was just the two of them swaying back and forth.

He looked down at her, moving a hand slowly from the dip of her back, up past her shoulder until his fingers found their way into the soft strands of her hair.

She purred for him the moment his fingertips grazed her scalp and the sound of her pleasure was so tempting, so damn powerful, it nearly overtook his senses.

His thumb grazed across one of her dangling ruby and diamond earrings he'd glimpsed when they'd met at the bar. They were a flash of fire and ice tied together in an intricate design where neither could be extricated from the other.

His body stiffened at the thought of their limbs being tangled together in a similar fashion. He internally chastised himself. He'd just met this woman. His needy response to her presence was a bit much, especially for a laid-back person like him who always went with the flow.

"You are the most exquisite being in this room tonight."

She smiled up at him, putting those sultry matte lips of hers on full display, making him fight their pull.

"I'm already dancing with you. You don't need to butter me up at this point."

He splayed his hand against the small curve in her back, looking down at her with all the intensity he could muster.

"I'm not trying to schmooze you."

"Then what are you trying to do, Mr. Phantom?"

"This."

It was the only warning he gave her as he leaned down, pressing his lips to hers. Although, it was somewhat of a chaste kiss—they were standing in the middle of the Texas Cattleman's Club after all, and he didn't need the busybodies of Royal reporting back to his mama about her youngest son pushing the boundaries of public appropriateness yet again. Even though it was just a peck, his flesh burned with need the moment his lips touched hers.

He wanted more, and with the way she moaned so beautifully, full of a powerful want that mirrored his own, he aimed to get as much of her as he could.

He was about to deepen the kiss when the music stopped and the lights came up just a bit. As lights brightened outside his closed lids, he could feel her pulling away from him. Not just to politely end their connection, but to free herself of his embrace.

"I'm sorry. I shouldn't have done that."

He could feel his brow pulling into a sharp V. "What, kiss me back? Trust me, darlin', I have no regrets about it. In fact, I was hoping we could do it again."

She stepped back, bringing a respectable amount of distance between them. There was something akin to panic in her eyes that set him on edge.

"I'm sorry. I have to go."

"Wait, did I do something wrong? Did I overstep?"

She shook her head, granting him a shaky smile.

"You did absolutely nothing wrong. It's just time for me to go."

As he attempted to step forward, he felt a hand grip his shoulder from behind, drawing his attention away. When he saw it was Vic interrupting, he turned away from his friend, but by then it was too late. His mystery lady was gone.

Jayden dropped his head, pinching the bridge of his nose as he tried to quell the annoyance at Vic growing in his belly.

"You have the worst damn timing, Vic."

When Jayden opened his eyes, the light glinted off of something sparkling on the floor. Bending down and scooping it up quickly with adept fingers, he recognized it instantly. Not only had his real-life Cinderella absconded from his embrace and his view, just like in the fairy tale, she'd left something behind.

"What's that?" Vic's fiancée Aubrey questioned, making Jayden aware of her presence for the first time.

"The only clue I have to figure out who the lady in red is behind her mask."

Vic gave him a remorseful look. "I'm sorry, man, I didn't mean to interrupt. I just wanted to show you how well our plan is working."

"Our plan?" Jayden folded his arms and tilted his head. "Don't blame this on me. This was all you, Vic. I just went along for the ride."

His friend shrugged, apparently too satisfied with

himself to notice Jayden wasn't exactly in the best of moods. Vic pointed to a far corner in the room where Ryan and Morgan seemed to be getting along quite nicely.

"That was almost too easy." Vic's gloating was beginning to get on Jayden's nerves. Not because he didn't want to see Morgan and Ryan happy together. If for no other reason than stopping their incessant bickering, Jayden would be thrilled if those two actually found their way to each other.

But in watching the two of them whispering closely together, Jayden could see all the possibilities of what could be, and it made something inside him ache with the need to explore his own possibilities with the stranger in red too.

"I hope it works out the way you want, Vic. But you're gonna have to deal with the rest of this on your own."

"What's going on, Jayden?"

Jayden rubbed his thumb across the large ruby at the bottom of the elongated earring as if it was a divining rod that could lead him to the one he wanted to be with.

"I have a Cinderella to find."

Three

"So, are you gonna drink that coffee or just stare at it? If it's the latter, let me just take it off your hands."

Jayden broke free of his daydream just in time to see his older brother, Jonathan, reaching for Jayden's coffee cup.

"Fratricide is a real thing. Don't make me have to show you."

Jonathan snatched his hand away from Jayden's cup with a snarky grin plastered on his face.

"You still 'round here moping because of your mystery lady? You sure she was even real? Maybe you had one too many cocktails at the club and you just imagined her."

"Did Vic and Morgan imagine her too? Because they saw her as well."

Jonathan's smile spread wider as his shoulders began to shake with laughter.

"What?" Jayden didn't bother trying to keep the annoyance out of his voice. Although it was usually the younger brother's prerogative to annoy his older sibling, right now, those roles were definitely reversed and Jayden didn't like it one bit.

"It's just, I've never actually seen you care this much about anything. You're always so laid-back and easygoing, without a care in the world. It's been three days since that masquerade ball and you can't stop obsessing over the 'red queen,' as you call her."

Jayden couldn't deny his brother's observation. There wasn't much that could get under his skin. He just wasn't built that way. But he couldn't deny the truth in Jonathan's statement. He was obsessing.

"I can't find anyone who knows who she is." He shoved his hand in the back pocket of his jeans, pulling the ruby and diamond earring free. "No one recognized her earring either. It's like she's disappeared."

Frustration coiled around his spine, making him sit straight on the breakfast bar stool.

"In a small town like Royal, where everybody knows everybody else's business, finding this woman shouldn't be this hard."

"Maybe she doesn't want to be found." His

brother's observation was logical, but methodical thinking wasn't what Jayden was going for right now.

"Then let her tell me that to my face. Until then, I'm gonna see if I can track Morgan down and get her to tell me anything. The red queen mentioned they were friends. I figure Morgan should know something. She wasn't around when I went by the Grandin ranch and she hasn't been answering her phone at the boutique. With as busy as she seems to be, I figure a surprise visit is the best way to catch up with her."

"Catch up with or interrogate her?"

Goodness his older brother was annoying.

"Probably a little of both." Jayden's honest answer made Jonathan shake his head with pity.

"I hope this woman turns out to be worth all this effort you're putting in. Because as tied up in knots as you seem to be over her, and as useless as you've been at doing ranch work since you met her, I'm afraid it will break you if you find a pumpkin instead of a queen."

"You and me both, Jonathan."

"Please stop pretending that bowl of chicken salad is so interesting you can't pay attention to me."

Zanai looked up from the colorful and leafy display of vegetables and protein at Morgan's interruption. She found her friend staring at her from across the table with a cat-who-ate-the-canary grin slapped on her pretty mouth.

"I haven't the slightest idea what you're talking about. You invited me out to lunch, I presumed I was supposed to eat."

"Lunch, my great-aunt Tilly," Morgan groused. "I'm sitting here trying to tell my best friend about my drunken escapades with Ryan, and your head is miles away."

Damn, Zanai certainly hadn't been listening if she'd missed that.

"You slept with Ryan?"

Ryan and Morgan fought like predators in the wild kingdom, each trying to assert their dominance as ruler of the land. The fact that Zanai hadn't soaked up every juicy detail meant her mind had to be on something else, or someone else, as it were in this case.

"Maybe I did. Maybe I didn't. You should've been listening."

Zanai bowed her head in deference to Morgan. "I'm so sorry, Morgan. I can't seem to keep my head on straight today. Please tell me this story again because I need to know how you and your mortal enemy ended up in bed…together…with neither of you killing the other."

Morgan's face beamed with mischief, which ratcheted up Zanai's need for the details.

"I never said we slept together. I said we had escapades. Most of which were fueled by alcohol," Morgan replied. "Lots of alcohol. But I'm not repeating

that story again until you give me the details on what
or who has you so distracted."

Zanai opened her mouth to deny the accusation in
Morgan's pointed gaze, but before she could come up
with anything to say, Morgan raised her manicured
finger to interrupt her.

"Three days, Zanai. It's been three days since
the masquerade ball here at the club. It's been three
whole days since I watched Jayden Lattimore kiss
you in the middle of the dance floor. I'm your best
friend. If anyone is supposed to get the scuttlebutt
about this, it's me. You can hold out on everyone
else, but not me."

Zanai closed her eyes briefly, shaking her head at
her friend's antics. "Careful, Morgan, you're sounding like one of the old gossips in this town."

"Since I have a vested interest in your well-being,
it's not gossip. It's concern for my oldest friend."

Zanai laughed at that. "I'm not your oldest friend.
My father didn't pack up my life in Brooklyn and
drop me off in this one-pony town until seventh
grade."

Morgan threw up her hands in mock frustration.
"Fine." She audibly exhaled for emphasis. "You're
not my oldest friend, just my dearest. And as such,
you owe me this. What happened? One minute one
of the richest and most eligible bachelors in Royal
was kissing you and the next you were running out

of the TCC so fast, you lost your very expensive ruby and diamond earring. Spill it."

Zanai dropped the fork in her hand and shifted in her seat. She'd tried hard to forget everything about her time at the ball, everything that reminded her of how awkward and out of place she really was.

"It was..." Zanai thought back to the handful of moments she'd spent with Jayden and sighed. "Magical."

Morgan gave a delighted squeal that had several people looking in their direction.

"Tell me everything," Morgan commanded.

"Jayden was funny and sweet, and so handsome, I could hardly notice anyone else in the room."

"I'm not surprised. Even when we were kids, he's always been a charmer."

Zanai wouldn't argue Morgan's point because as smooth as that man was, his talents for making a woman feel as if she were the only person in the room had to be cultivated from birth.

"Being in front of a man like that has always—"

"A man like what?" She let Morgan's question hang in the air unanswered. A mistake on her part. It only gave her friend fuel to keep going.

"Zanai, please tell me how Jayden is different from any other man in Royal?"

"He's wealthy, he's handsome, he has status in the town."

"Zanai, you do realize your father is one of the richest men in town?"

She leaned back in her chair, part of her resolve bleeding away at the mention of her father.

"Yes, Morgan. My father is very rich. But Jayden's family has old money wealth. We're two different classes of people in the eyes of most folk in this town. My father couldn't buy the prestige and respect the Lattimores have, and trust me, he's tried."

"You really have to get over this nonsense, Zanai. You've been in Royal for fifteen years now. You belong here. Stop letting the snobs in this town tell you otherwise."

That was much easier said than done. Zanai had been reminded from the moment she stepped foot in Royal that she didn't belong. Between the people in town treating her like an afterthought and her father and stepmother constantly reminding her of why she didn't measure up to everyone else, being a resident of Royal hadn't been easy for Zanai at all.

"I know you can't see it, Morgan. Your beauty, your old money and, to some degree, your race give you status in this town. To your circle, it doesn't matter how much money my father makes. I'm still the Black girl from Brooklyn invading their social club. I'll never measure up."

Morgan flipped a long tendril of red hair over her shoulder. It was a clear sign she was gearing up for a fight. Well, that and the angry blush she could see creeping up Morgan's neck to her face.

"I don't give a damn what anyone says or thinks. You're the best thing that's ever happened to this town. You belong here. And as progressive as Royal is, I know this is still Texas, so I'm not blind to how unpleasantly narrow-minded some of our residents are."

Morgan's eyes locked on hers with flecks of fire dancing in them. This was her protective mode. Morgan was a fighter, and she always fought for those she cared most about.

"Being so closely tied to the Lattimores over the years, it's almost impossible to not see how race plays a role in status in this town. I've had a front row seat to some of the downright horrible things people say and do. But those people don't matter. You do. And the way Jayden kept his eyes on you all night, I'd say you matter very much to him too. So stop with this 'I don't belong' nonsense. It seemed like you were into whatever was happening between you and Jayden. What happened to change your mind?"

Obviously, they weren't going to get past this because Morgan wasn't going to drop it. Deep down, Zanai couldn't be upset. She'd kissed one of the princes of Royal at the ball. It was probably the closest thing to a fairy tale she'd ever experience. Of course she wanted to share the magic of that moment with her best friend.

"You're right. Jayden is a charmer. But more than that. There's this quiet intensity about him that's so noticeable. He doesn't seem to care about what the rest of the world is thinking, and in our circles, that's so refreshing. To be the focus of that intensity, it was…intoxicating."

"Then why run away?"

"Jayden didn't recognize me at the ball. And even if he did, he only knows me peripherally through you. We've never actually had a conversation. No matter how much money my father has, I'll never be a socialite. All I care about are the kids from work. My idea of a fun night is starting a new book. I'd bore Jayden to death. So, when he kissed me, I decided to end it there so our stark differences couldn't ruin it later. Most people in this town think I'm a shy weirdo. After that kiss, I just couldn't bear the thought of Jayden thinking that too."

Morgan slid her hand across the table to clasp Zanai's, lending her comfort and strength the way she always did.

"We both know there's nothing shy about you. You're reserved because some really nasty people have shown you how little appreciation they have for your interests and talents. That's not your fault. It's theirs."

She squeezed Zanai's hand and offered her a concerned smile.

"You've protected yourself and there's nothing

wrong with that. I just worry that in your quest to keep the asshats away, you're going to miss out on knowing a really great person like Jayden, and more importantly, you'll rob him of the opportunity of getting to know someone as wonderful as you."

Morgan's warmth cloaked Zanai like a familiar, fuzzy blanket. The chill of her fears dissipating underneath its comfort made her count her blessings for Morgan Grandin's presence in her life.

Zanai was about to say as much when she glanced up and saw the subject of their discussion entering the club.

"Oh, my goodness, Morgan. Did you set this up?"

"Set what up?"

Morgan turned her head to see what Zanai was referring to. Zanai could tell the exact moment her friend zeroed in on the intended target because when Morgan brought her attention back to Zanai, that wicked grin of hers was back with a vengeance.

"Morgan, did you tell Jayden to meet us here?"

The woman shook her head. "No, I didn't. But I certainly wish I had the forethought to do so. This is about to get interesting."

"No, it's not." Zanai spoke through clenched teeth, trying hard to keep her voice from rising above a whisper.

Morgan was about to say something else, but by the time she was able to speak another word, Jayden was standing at their table smiling down at them with the same wicked grin he'd worn for most of their interaction at the ball. Only this time, half his face wasn't covered with a mask and she bore its mesmerizing full strength.

"Afternoon, ladies. I'm sorry to interrupt your meal, but if I may, I need Morgan's help with something."

The tension in Zanai's body relaxed just a bit. He wasn't here for her. That should be a relief, and to some degree it was. But more than anything, disappointment began to set in and she realized a big part of her wanted him to be looking for her.

Jayden shoved his hand in his pocket, and then opened a flat palm in front of Morgan. "Would you happen to know who owns this?"

Jayden glanced at Morgan as he waited for her answer. There was a flash of recognition and mischief in her eyes that made him hopeful he was closer to finding his Cinderella.

"Yes, I know exactly who you mean."

Zanai was sipping from a large glass of water and quickly began coughing.

"You okay, Zanai?"

He intended the question as a cursory politeness, something you do automatically when you see someone having a bit of difficulty. But then she watched him for a long pause before answering. "I'm fine. Water just went down the wrong way."

He stared intently at Zanai, which was something altogether different. With her long and wavy dark hair and deep brown complexion with reddish undertones, it was difficult not to recognize her beauty. A beauty that seemed to call to him, transfix him to the point that he felt ensnared, trapped in its presence and unable to do anything but let his sight linger upon her.

She dropped her gaze to the offending glass of water sitting in front of her and it was the only reason her hold over him loosened.

Jayden shook his head, trying to get his bearings. He'd known or rather known of this woman for fifteen years. Never had he felt so drawn to her. Never had he noticed just how captivating the depth of her dark brown eyes were or how tempting the graceful line of her neck was.

Zanai had always been a bit standoffish for his taste. Almost every time he'd encountered her, she'd had her nose in a book as if she couldn't be bothered to interact with the people around her. Her tendency to be so serious always left him cold, so he'd never taken the opportunity to say more than *hi* and *bye* when in her presence.

Today was different, however. There was something different about the way she looked at him. It was as if she were finally seeing him and allowing him to see her.

"Jayden, you were asking about who that earring belongs to?"

Morgan's voice barely registered as he stared into Zanai's deep brown eyes. There was a familiarity there that went beyond the very casual acquaintance they'd shared over the years. It was strong, tethering him to her, nearly blocking his senses from detecting all other stimuli.

"Ah, yeah," he answered as he closed his eyes attempting to mentally set himself free from Zanai's hold. "While we were dancing, she—"

He intended to glance down at the earring in his hand when he saw the light breaking through the wall of nearby windows glint off of Zanai's wrist.

There, accentuating her delicate wrist was a ruby and diamond bracelet that looked eerily similar to the lost earring he had in his hand. He was no jeweler, but the cut, color and setting of the stones, the platinum metal, the resemblance was too great to ignore.

"It was you."

Zanai looked up at him with a mix of fear and disbelief in her eyes.

"What was me?"

"Zanai, you're the red queen."

She sat there with her eyes wide and her mouth open, and Jayden knew instantly that he wasn't wrong. He'd known that from the moment he spotted her bracelet, but her expression of shocked disbelief gave it all away.

She tried to recover, shaking her head and look-ing as if she were about to mount a defense for his accusation. But when he held the matching earring next to the bracelet on her wrist, they both knew her charade was over.

"Why'd you run out like that?"

He tilted his head in expectation of an answer. However, Zanai couldn't seem to find her words if her hanging jaw was any indication.

"I wasn't feeling well and Zanai was kind enough to take me home." Morgan's excuse wasn't enough to pull his attention away from Zanai. Even though he was about to reply to Morgan, he kept his gaze firmly locked onto Zanai's bewildered face.

"Didn't I see you with Ryan later that evening?" He reached for his phone, pulling it out and making a display of looking through his contacts. "I could always call Ryan and see if I'm mistaken or not."

Morgan gave him the same nervous smile she did when they were kids and he'd caught her play-ing with his video games without permission. She was busted and she knew it.

"Well," Morgan's voice cut through their fixed gazes. "It seems like you two have a lot to talk about. I'm just gonna slip out and leave the two of you alone."

When neither of them said anything, Morgan stood, smiling as she looked back and forth between him and Zanai. "I'll call later tonight, Zanai."

When she was standing beside Jayden, she playfully swatted him on the arm. "You'd better behave."

Without taking his eyes off Zanai, he nodded. After the way she'd run off at the ball, he couldn't afford to let her out of his sight for fear she'd run again. Although he knew that wasn't the only reason he couldn't take his eyes off of her.

There was something drawing him to her. Something primal, pulling at his insides, making him hyperaware of everything from the tempting way her long lashes fluttered against the smooth brown skin of her cheeks, to the short, quiet breaths she took as she stared back at him.

He let a few long seconds pass after Morgan's departure before he sat in the seat across from Zanai.

"Ja-Jayden," she stammered. "There's been some mistake."

He held up a hand to stop whatever it was she thought she was doing with what appeared to be a half-assed explanation in the works.

"The only mistake was letting you get away from me. I just need to know one thing, Zanai."

She swallowed, her eyes still wide with the surprise of discovery.

"What's that?"

"Why you left?" He watched her in silence before speaking again. "I need to know why you ran away from me at the ball."

Four

"Mr. Lattimore, if you'll be joining Dr. James, would you like me to bring you a menu?"

Jayden briefly tore his eyes from Zanai's face to be polite and answer the server standing at their table.

"No, thank you," he replied. "I won't be staying long."

When they were alone again, he tapped his fingers on the table waiting for Zanai to fill the empty silence spreading between them.

"As I said, I don't plan on being here long, but that doesn't mean I'm leaving without an answer. What happened three days ago, Zanai? You spent the night flirting with me, and then after I kissed you, you ran off. What kind of game were you playing?"

She was barefaced except for soft pink lip gloss that reminded him of how kissable her lips were. Simple elegance was how he'd describe her. So beautiful without any enhancements that she was absolutely stunning when she wore makeup and adorned herself in finery.

How he hadn't noticed how striking she was before this moment was beyond him. Perhaps it was because his ego had taken a hit when she'd run off at the ball. Or maybe his sisterly view of Morgan had blinded him to how attractive he found her. Whatever it was, he was mentally kicking himself for not noticing how lovely she was.

"I wasn't playing a game."

He lifted his brow, calling her on her lie without saying a word.

"Okay, fine," she capitulated, throwing up her hands before placing them quietly against the table. "I was playing a game and I'm sorry it was at your expense. I just got caught up."

He leaned in. "In what, exactly?"

Her gaze drifted from his and she focused on a single spot on the table instead. "In the feeling of having someone desire me, be so interested in me he'd seek me out in a crowded room and try to monopolize my time."

She shrugged, lifting her eyes and face to him

so he could see a slightly embarrassed blush coloring her cheeks.

"Men like you don't look at women like me that way. Being treated like that was intoxicating."

He shook his head. Something in her tone rubbed him the wrong way and it annoyed him that he couldn't quite pinpoint what it was.

"Men like me, women like you, what the hell are you talking about, Zanai? We've known each other for years."

"Yeah," she replied. "But in all the time we've known each other, we've never spoken more than a handful of words at a time. We're best friends with siblings, but we hardly know each other at all. Up until I put on some makeup, a mask and a red dress, you hardly knew I existed. Hell, as close as we were on that dance floor, you didn't even recognize me. That's how invisible I've been to you all these years."

He sat straighter in his chair carefully processing what she was saying. "You can't call me shallow for not recognizing you in one breath and put yourself down in the next. What the hell, Zanai?"

She tucked her bottom lip between her teeth and every muscle in his body clenched with need as she swiped the pink tip of her tongue across it, seemingly soothing where her teeth had gently scraped across her skin.

What he wouldn't give to press his lips to hers again.

"I'm not trying to insult you and I'm not putting myself down. It's just a fact. I'm not your type. I'm not most people's type. I get that. It was just nice to see how the other half lives for once. I'm sorry if I got a little carried away by letting you kiss me."

She wasn't wrong about not being his type. She was intellectual, an academic. She did important work. That wasn't to say he wasn't attracted to smart, professional women. He certainly was. But Zanai always seemed as if she wasn't concerned with dating and social activities.

He'd thought it was because she was shy. But after spending time with her at the ball, he wasn't so sure that was the case. It dawned on him that maybe she was so distant because she didn't think anyone wanted to be close to her.

"I'll accept your apology if you accept mine."

Her brow furrowed as she let her curious gaze slide down his face.

"What on earth do you have to apologize for?"

"For not recognizing how absolutely alluring you are until three days ago."

Her eyes went wide, blinking repeatedly as she appeared to digest what he was saying. He had to admit, since Zanai was always in control, always so focused, it was empowering to know he could knock her off her game like this. He liked it so much, he figured he should keep the game going as long as he could.

"Let me rectify my mistake. Have dinner with me, Zanai."

She opened her mouth to speak. It took a few tries, but she finally figured out how to push air through her vocal cords and produce sound.

"Are you asking me out on a date?"

"Indeed, I am."

"When?"

He leaned in, brandishing the lopsided grin his granny called sweeter than sugar. "The sooner the better. Tonight."

He was about to stand up when she reached across the table to grip his arm. He wore a long-sleeved button-down shirt, but even through the material, he could feel the heat of her touch burning through to his skin.

"Jayden, you can't just ask me out to dinner. I mean, we've known each other for fifteen years and have never shown any interest in each other. This doesn't make any sense."

This was a sight to behold. The cool Dr. Zanai James flustered and out of her element. He could definitely get used to this.

"Zanai, I didn't appreciate brussels sprouts when I was sixteen either. That doesn't mean my tastes haven't matured as a thirty-one-year-old man. You're a gorgeous, accomplished woman. Why wouldn't I or any man be interested in you?"

She shook her head as dismay threaded her brows.

"You were attracted to a costume, Jayden. Not the woman in it. That wasn't the real me."

"I don't believe that."

She stared at him open-mouthed with her tongue stuck to the roof of her mouth.

"Sure, the costume is what caught my attention. I don't think I've ever seen a more beautiful vision than you in that red dress. But it was the conversation and the banter that made me want to know the woman in the dress more."

He reached across the table, placing a gentle hand over hers before lightly squeezing it in his palm. The feel of her, even in this very unsexy way, stoked his desire like gasoline poured onto a wildfire.

"I think, maybe for the first time, you were being more you than you've ever been. That costume gave you the freedom to let the real Zanai come out to play. And quite frankly, I want to spend more time getting to know that woman.

"Meet me at Sheen tonight for dinner. My friend Charlotte is the chef there. I'm sure she can get us a table even on such short notice."

With a quick widening of her eyes, she scanned him as if she was trying to figure out how to fit the pieces of his puzzle together.

"You're serious about this? You want to go on an actual date with me?"

"Darlin', there are only a few things in life I'm serious about. My family, my friends and my food are of the greatest importance to me. If I'm inviting you to share in either, it's a pretty big deal. What do you say?"

She gave him one more assessing look before one corner of her sexy mouth curved into a half smile.

"I say yes."

"Why on earth did I let you talk me into this?"

Zanai could hear Morgan's amused giggle coming through her AirPods as she smoothed nervous hands down the front of her dress.

"I wasn't even in the room when you accepted Jayden's invitation. How is this my fault?"

"If you hadn't pushed me to attend that stupid ball, we never would've run into each other in the first place."

"Not true," Morgan countered with her blunt, matter-of-fact tone. "You're at my house and around my family all the time. You would've run into Jayden casually like you have any other time. Only this time, you couldn't hide away in my room like you usually do."

"I have no idea what you're talking about. I don't hide from Jayden. We've barely spoken to each other over the fifteen years I've been in Royal."

Yes, they both had a connection to the Grandin family, but that didn't make the two of them friends. They were friends of friends, who nodded hello whenever they crossed paths.

"Jayden has barely noticed me in all this time. He's never paid me much mind. The only reason he's interested now is you put me in a dress that made my cleavage look awesome."

Morgan's loud sigh, a sign that Zanai was testing her patience, seeped through the phone. "News flash, you have great cleavage. You couldn't hide it even if you were wearing a turtleneck. Accept it, the only thing that put you on Jayden's radar was the fact that you looked him in the eye and said more than your compulsory 'Hello, Jayden' when you saw him. You let him see what I've always known, you're pretty great. So, stop being nervous and go out there and have a good time. You can do this. But more importantly, you want to do this."

Zanai inhaled slowly through her nose then exhaled through pursed lips, trying to calm herself down. Morgan was right, she did want to do this.

She took another look at herself in the mirror. Fashion had never been her forte. She didn't know what was in season or on trend. But the simple fitted LBD with the square neckline and spaghetti straps accented her modest curves.

"Just be yourself, Zanai."

If she were going to be herself, something was missing from this outfit. She walked over to the corner where her cardigans hung and pulled a red one off the rack. When she glanced at her reflection in the mirror, she felt a sense of calm wash over her.

She looked fashionable, like she was comfortable in her own skin.

If this evening had a prayer of being moderately successful, she needed to be herself. Well, the parts of her that weren't awkward and standoffish. She wasn't ashamed of those parts of her personality. Unfortunately, those traits kept people away, and as she stood there smiling at herself in the mirror, she realized she didn't want to push Jayden away.

Besides, the few moments she'd spent pretending to be the belle of the ball were exhausting. There was no way she could keep that up for an extended period of time. Tonight, for better or worse, Jayden Lattimore would get to meet the real Zanai James, whoever that was.

"Morgan?"

"Yes."

"Thank you for always pushing me to exist in the world we live in. I know I don't make it easy, but I appreciate it. No matter how tonight turns out, I don't regret going to that ball. I got to be Cinderella for a night. Who could be mad at that?"

"Well, well, well." Jonathan nearly sang the words coming out of his mouth. "Look at the number two son."

Jayden walked into the kitchen looking for his older brother. He found Jonathan standing in the center of the room leaning against the large granite counter with Alexa and Caitlyn flanking him on each side.

"Wow." Alexa walked over to Jayden, walking around him in a circle as she assessed him. "You're actually wearing something other than jeans and cowboy boots?" She waved her hand up and down, noting the button-down shirt, blazer, slacks and dress shoes he wore. "Where exactly are you going?"

Jayden was about to say something smart to his younger sister, but the lawyer in her would have an even better comeback so he didn't bother. He realized she wasn't exactly wrong in her observation. Jayden reserved dress clothes for weddings, funerals and events held at the Texas Cattleman's Club.

His family's business was the land they lived on, making his office attire of a T-shirt or a plaid shirt, jeans and broken-in cowboy boots his go-to. But the usual wouldn't do for tonight.

"Who you getting cute for?" Caitlyn stepped over to where Jayden and Alexa stood.

"Are you here again? Don't you have your own place? A whole man to get back to? Where's Dev anyway?" Jayden asked.

"He'll be here in a few minutes." Her reply was quick and served with a wide grin. "Now back to you. What's with the outfit?"

Jonathan responded, "He's got a date with Zanai James."

"Zanai?" Alexa echoed, tilting her head to the side

as she looked up at Jayden. "Morgan's friend? You're actually going out with her tonight?"

Jayden stepped around his sisters, heading for the center of the room where his brother stood. "What's that supposed to mean, Alexa?"

She shrugged, sharing a knowing glance with their sister before turning her dark brown eyes back to him.

"She's not exactly your type, Jayden?"

"What exactly are you trying to say about Zanai?" Alexa was bold. She didn't ever mince words, so he was certain she wouldn't hold back on an explanation. But as he waited for her to speak, he could feel the slight twinge of something dark growing inside him, daring his sister to say anything bad about Zanai.

"She's quiet and rarely does anything to draw any attention to herself. She's a lovely woman, no doubt. But kind of reserved for your tastes, don't you think?"

He could feel his body tensing, gearing up for an argument he didn't want to have. Usually, he'd just ignore Alexa. But tonight, her observations annoyed the hell out of him.

"Watch your mouth, Alexa."

His sister raised up her hands in surrender and softened her voice as she walked over to where he was standing.

"Hey, that's not a slight against Zanai. It's more

of an observation of your dating practices. You don't go for the quiet girls. You like 'em loud, brash and ready to have fun at the drop of a hat. As little as I know about her, that for certain isn't Zanai."

Jayden nodded as the anger bled out of him. "You're right, she's usually quiet. But I got a glimpse of the fun person she's been hiding all these years. I think deep down, that's the real Zanai."

"So, what, you plan to dig deep until you get to the real her?" Caitlyn's question drew his gaze to hers across the room.

"Yeah," he confirmed. "I think all she needs is someone to give her a little encouragement and show her how to have fun."

His brother chuckled and his sisters groaned in unison.

"And let me guess—" Alexa stepped closer "—you're that someone? You're the man that's going to teach her how to be one of the cool kids in Royal?"

He nodded. That was exactly his plan.

"What is this?" Alexa continued with a tinge of heat in her voice. "The Royal edition of *She's All That*, but with Black people?" She huffed, walking away from him as she shook her head. "You can't change who a person is with a makeover, Jayden. And I worry if Zanai would want to date a man who wanted to change her into something he thought was more suitable."

He could see Alexa's point, but somehow his plan hadn't sounded as superficial in his head.

"Don't act like women don't do the same thing. How many times have I heard you and Caitlyn talk about a woman upgrading a man? How is this any different?"

His sister narrowed her gaze and pointed it at him like a sharp dagger. If he were a smart man, which he obviously wasn't for even attempting to have this conversation with both his sisters in the room, he would've kept his mouth shut, gotten the keys to his brother's car like he'd intended and headed out to meet Zanai. But today he chose stupidity, so here they were.

"Let me tell you something, big brother." He inwardly cringed. Any time Alexa began a sentence with that phrase, it meant she was about slay you with her sharp tongue. "When a woman upgrades a man, he consciously changes because he wants to be worthy of her, and the enhancements are usually something external like his wardrobe or his status. You're talking about fundamentally changing someone's personality so she can be worthy of you and meet your superficial standards for your arm candy. That's not the same thing."

Caitlyn nodded, walking closer to their sister, standing in solidarity. "Alexa is right, Jay. Zanai isn't a piece of clay for you to mold. She's a real person. If you're not into her as she is, you might want to leave her alone. No one likes to feel unworthy."

There was something about the way Caitlyn spoke that made Jayden wonder if she had any personal experience with the topic at hand. The thought that someone had made his baby sister feel unworthy raked against something in him. Luckily Caitlyn now had Dev who treated her like a queen.

Did he see the hypocrisy in his reaction? Absolutely. But that was his right as a big brother to be protective of his younger sisters no matter the circumstances.

"Thank you for the lecture, ladies. However, all I came in here for were the keys to Jonathan's Bentley. If I stay here any longer, I'll be late."

His brother dangled the keys in the air and Jayden grabbed them as he made a hasty exit. Just as he was about to step out of the kitchen, he heard Alexa's voice filling the air.

"Zanai is a person, Jayden, not a pet project. Remember that when you're trying to make her more suitable for you to date."

He pretended not to hear her as he continued his trek out of the kitchen and down the hall, which eventually opened into the foyer. As he stepped through the door, for a split second, he wondered if he shouldn't call the whole thing off. At that moment, his phone vibrated in his pocket notifying him of a text from Zanai.

Leaving now. Can't wait to see you there.

His stomach sank. His sisters were right. This woman was too innocent for the likes of him. But the idea of her waiting with anticipation for him stroked his ego in a way he couldn't ignore. He was a bastard. That was for certain. But he would be the lucky bastard spending time with one Zanai James, and he wouldn't turn that down for all the guilt in the world.

He tapped out a quick message before heading for his brother's car in the circular driveway.

OMW. Looking forward to seeing you too.

Five

Zanai sat quietly in the waiting area of the restaurant. She was a tad early and their table wasn't ready yet.

Overeager much, Zanai?

Was she already coming off as desperate? Their date hadn't even started yet and she was already being weird.

This was a mistake. She stood up, intending to march right out of the restaurant, get her keys from the valet and run away before Jayden could get there. But as she turned toward the door, she saw Jayden's solid body fill the entrance and somehow her feet wouldn't obey the signals from her brain screaming for her to run.

"Zanai." His voice was deep and smooth like a fine scotch poured over ice. He took in the sight of her. She could feel his tantalizing gaze sliding down every inch of her body. "You look…amazing."

His last word hung in the air as he continued his appraisal, swiping his tongue against his bottom lip as if he'd found a mouthwatering treat.

"Th-thank you." She cleared her throat, hoping that her stammer appeared more like the result of a pending cough rather than the bellyful of nerves currently dancing in her abdomen.

"Have you been waiting long?"

She shook her head. "Only about five minutes. I'm obsessive about punctuality, so don't worry."

He didn't respond, not verbally anyway. Instead, he let his gaze openly pass over her again. He looked hungry. And if she wasn't imagining things, he was hungry for her.

Zanai hadn't had a stable of men in her life. She'd dated a few, but nothing serious ever came of their brief associations. Before now, she'd never witnessed a man look at her with so much desire that she could almost feel his heated stare licking at her skin.

"Mr. Lattimore, welcome back to Sheen." A young man dressed in a high-end suit stood next to them, breaking the spell Jayden was weaving around her. "Your table is ready, sir. Would you and the lady mind following me?"

Jayden simply nodded, putting his hand at the

small of her back. It was a simple gesture, one he'd probably made thousands of times with the women he knew. But it nearly short-circuited her brain, leaving her unable to do more than fall in step beside him.

The host sat them in a corner booth which, coupled with the dim lighting of the room, gave them privacy. She was grateful. The last thing she needed was the vicious Royal rumor mill getting wind of whatever this was happening between them.

She gently chewed on the inside of her cheek trying to squash that idea as soon as it tried to form. There was nothing happening between them. Jayden was fascinated with a dress, makeup and a fancy hairdo. Free of those things, he'd quickly get bored with her like everyone else did.

"Everything okay?" His voice reached her first, followed by the warm sensation of his large palm surrounding her hand. The satisfying heat traveled through her skin, infusing her blood, and spread throughout her body like hot tea on a blistering cold day in Europe or the Northeast.

"Yes." She managed to shake herself free of the daze his touch invoked. "Why do you ask?"

He let his gaze slide down her face as if he were trying to assess more than her words. "You're just different than you were at the ball."

The red flags her fear had tried so hard to warn her about were snapping hard in the metaphorical wind. She'd been waiting for this. It was the obvious result for anyone who'd been paying attention.

"The ball was make-believe. I played dress-up and danced with the most eligible prince in Royal. But at the stroke of midnight, my fairy godmother's magic wore off and I turned back into a pumpkin. That's usually what happens in fairy tales. Why are you so surprised?"

She waited for the awkward discomfort that usually followed when people realized she didn't possess the ability to engage in polite small talk. But to her surprise, Jayden didn't shrink back. Instead, he simply nodded.

At first, she thought he was agreeing with her and a little bit of sadness slightly quelled the happy buzz she'd had all day. But as a spark of mischief filled his dark eyes and his lips bent into a cocky grin, she realized he wasn't agreeing with her at all.

"I call bullshit."

Her eyes widened. Not at his use of profanity, but that he didn't seem to be distancing himself as expected. Instead, he leaned in, locking his amused stare with hers before sliding his thumb over the back of her hand.

"On what exactly?"

"I don't think any of that nonsense about you turning into a pumpkin is true. What I saw in you the night of the ball can't be faked. I think that was the real Zanai James finally escaping from the aloof, distant prison you keep her locked in."

She'd spent years learning how to keep her face expressionless when she heard things that shocked her. But sitting here in front of Jayden's penetrative gaze, she was finding it hard to keep her features schooled into a neutral palette that gave nothing away.

"You know, if I didn't know any better, I'd think you'd earned a PsyD right along with me. That was some first-class psychobabble right there."

"You would know, Dr. James, wouldn't you? That deflection tactic was top-grade. It's obvious I'm dealing with a pro."

"My professional abilities aside, it still doesn't make anything you're saying about me true. I'm not the woman you spent a few moments with at the masquerade ball. She doesn't exist."

He leaned back in his chair, still smoothing his thumb gently along the back of her hand. The motion was rhythmic and soothing, distracting her from the nerves she knew she should have in a situation like this.

"Oh, I beg to differ." His smile brightened and she found herself responding in kind, like her face muscles were somehow in sync with his, obeying his commands instead of hers.

"Do you, now?"

"I do. In fact, I think she does exist. I think she's

the real you. This watered-down facsimile of you is who you pretend to be, although I'm not sure why."

Her free hand cut through the air in a dismissive wave. "Seems you've got me all figured out then. What will we do with the rest of our evening if you've discovered all my hidden quirks in the first ten minutes of our night?"

He leaned in, his smile relaying something powerful with just a tinge of naughtiness. He lifted her hand to his mouth and graced her knuckles with a delicate kiss.

"Don't worry." His eyes burned with restrained passion and she had to remind herself they were in a public place. The intensity of his gaze was like a match to kindling, searing her entire body with the blaze of one look. "I'm sure I can come up with something."

She swallowed trying to push the difficult knot sitting at the back of her throat down so she could manage to speak.

"Your theory that I have some inner princess trapped within is unfounded. I don't mean to let you down, but I'm a boring plain Jane. From my ponytail to my barely there pink lip gloss, I'm as predictable as they come."

"But what if you're wrong?" His query was like a sledgehammer to her midsection, making her instinctually want to fold her frame in half. "And for the record, I don't think you have an inner princess. I think you're a full-blown monarch in your own right."

If nothing else, this man was good at telling a woman what she wanted to hear. Because even she couldn't deny how much she wanted his words to be true.

"What if you do have a queen inside that just hasn't been convinced to come out to play yet?"

She nodded, not because she agreed with him. The most interesting thing about Zanai was her name, and she wasn't responsible for that. If her late mother had known how bookish and uninterested in society her only daughter would be, she was sure *Zanai* wouldn't have been the moniker the new mother had chosen.

"Hear me out before you completely dismiss my theory. I think the reason your queen was on full display that night was because your majestic side was given a chance to be free. Once she was free, everyone around you, most of all me, had no choice but to be awestruck."

She had to admit, she liked his theory a lot better than her own. But there was no way she could buy into it. She knew herself too well to believe that kind of magic existed in her.

"So, because I dressed like a queen and felt like a queen, people treated me as if I was a queen? It sounds good, but I don't buy it. It's too preposterous to be true."

"It is true. And if you give me the chance to remind you of what it was like to be that queen, remind you of who you really are, I have no doubt her majesty will appear again."

She shook her head. What he was saying made absolutely no sense. But even still, his words had sparked something bright and impossible to ignore inside. There, where there was once quiet reserve, now burned a new, fiery hope. A hope she wasn't entirely certain she could ignore anymore, especially not when he was looking at her with his perfect, sexy smile and smoldering eyes.

She cleared her throat. "I'm afraid you're going to walk away from our time together disappointed."

"Doubtful," he countered. His shoulders were stiff with conviction and his smile beamed with confidence. He believed every word he was saying. This wasn't an act. "And after we finish our meal, I plan to convince you to follow me home so I can prove it."

She stared openly at him. Not because she was offended, quite the opposite. She was completely taken in by the possibility of what he was proposing and hoping in the end he was right.

"This is a beautiful view. So many stars tonight." Jayden leaned against the railing of his condo's balcony in the city proper as he watched Zanai take in the evening sky.

"I love ranch life. The open space, the working with your hands, the backbreaking labor, all of it gets my blood running. But the twinkle of a night sky in the city is somehow soothing to me."

The corners of her mouth tugged until a full-blown smile spread across her lips. "The quiet at night was the hardest thing for me to adjust to when I moved here from Brooklyn. Listening to all the crickets chirping so loudly kept me up all night."

She kept her gaze focused on the night sky, but he could see her smile dimming slightly even from her profile.

"We moved here very soon after my mother died. I'm sure my insomnia had more to do with that than the crickets, but still. Those little buggers wouldn't let me get any sleep. It's why I used to beg my father to take me with him whenever he had to travel for business. That noise, no matter if we were in Tokyo, Paris or London, there was always this buzz that soothed me."

"I didn't know you traveled so much."

"Yeah, it was one of the reasons I never really bonded with any other kids here besides Morgan. I was never really around. I just wanted to be with my dad. He hadn't remarried at the time, so he took me with him."

"What about school?"

"His business was on the rise by then. He wasn't as wealthy as he is now, but he could afford private tutors. They made sure I kept up with my work when I was away from school."

She looked up at him, a somber cloud draped over her face even when she attempted to share a forced smile with him.

"It wasn't all bad, if that's what you're thinking. I'd traveled most of the world by the time I was eighteen and I learned to speak several languages by immersing myself in other cultures versus reading a textbook. To tell you the truth, the only thing I missed about this town was Morgan."

Standing there in the moonlight, her beauty was breathtaking. But the stoic grace she used to hide her pain drew him to her, made him want to bring her joy to shove away the clouds that hung over her.

He lifted a finger to a loose tendril of hair blowing in the warm, gentle breeze of the night. "Hopefully, I can make you see there's more to miss about this town than Morgan."

She turned to him then, her gaze penetrating through his defenses and finding its way to the buried parts of him he'd never let a woman see. His association with women was about fun. Never anything of substance, never real. But the way her gaze burrowed through him until it hit something solid and consequential had him questioning his own good sense.

"Oh, yeah? What else is there besides Morgan?"

"Not *what*," he answered, "but *who*. Morgan's your friend. Hopefully there's some space in your life for a new friend like me."

A light bubble of laughter escaped her lips, bringing a softness to her features he hadn't been able to detect in the restaurant.

"We've known each other for fifteen years. I think that disqualifies you as *new*."

"We've spent a handful of moments together through mutual acquaintances, Zanai. That hardly counts as friendship. Admit it, we've never taken the time to really get to know each other. I think it might be fun to give it a try now."

She turned to the Royal skyline again, taking a break from whatever this game was the two of them were playing. He understood her need to distance herself. If she were feeling any of the desire and pull that he was, taking a moment to attempt to break the spell was the prudent thing to do.

"Fun seems to be important to you. You've got a reputation for being a 'good time' guy in Royal."

She turned around, staring directly at him at first before allowing her gaze to dip slightly. That wasn't a slip—everything he knew about Zanai spoke to her being very intentional. The words she spoke were careful and precise. Even when she was behind a mask, her words were almost as exact as a surgeon's scalpel. So that slip of her gaze wasn't anything to ignore. Brief though it was, he'd bet everything he owned that the good, sensible Dr. James was checking him out.

"Darlin' I'm not *a* 'good time' guy. I'm *the* 'good

time' guy. No one in this town can show you a better time than me."

"So, you're not proposing anything serious? Just fun, right?"

He stepped closer to her, seeing some unrecognizable thing in her eyes that made him want to be nearer. He lifted his hand, cupping her cheek, and softly stroked the skin beneath his thumb. It was something he'd done to women a million times before. But when she closed her eyes and leaned into his touch, everything about this moment felt new to him.

He'd known going into this Zanai wouldn't be like his other conquests. Their mutual connections to the Grandins meant he had to tread carefully to some degree. The last thing he needed was Morgan pissed at him for breaking her best friend's heart.

"Zanai, I'm not a playboy. I don't seek to collect women and I don't treat them poorly. My grandmother, mom and sisters would have my hide if I did, and trust me, I don't need that kind of stress in my life. But when I find a woman I like, and if she's willing to have a little fun, I'm all for showing her the best time I can."

The playful smile on her face eased the tension the turn of the conversation had brought. Something he was certainly relieved about.

"Are you close to the women in your family? The

few interactions I've had with the Lattimores, it always seemed like you were a close bunch."

"We're all pretty tight. My dad and brother too. Even my grandfather, although he sometimes forgets." For the Lattimores, it was them against the world. Not that they didn't form cherished relationships outside of their kinship—the Grandins were proof of that. But the Lattimores always supported each other, no matter what.

"Even though my siblings can be a pain and always give me crap, I couldn't imagine my life without the three of them. But you've got sisters, so I'm sure you get what I'm talking about."

"I wouldn't exactly say that."

There was a cautious but distant look in her eye that immediately drew his concern.

"I'm fifteen years older than my half sisters"

"Half sisters? People still make those kinds of distinctions about family?"

It was only after the thought leapt out of his mouth that he realized his words might come off as insensitive. But the slight pallor of sadness that briefly cloaked the brightness in her deep brown eyes wouldn't let him deviate from the conversation.

"My stepmother does." Her response was spoken in a matter-of-fact manner. But again, the distant look on her face made him think this was much more important than she was relaying.

"There's friction between you and your stepmother?"

She looked back over the skyline, seemingly needing to break away from his prying gaze. "Not like you think. We're not mortal enemies or anything like that. I've just never been her priority. I'm a reminder that she isn't the first Mrs. James and she doesn't like playing second fiddle to anyone. She and Sanford really focus on the family they've created together. I've never really fit into that dynamic so well."

Again, her delivery was very benign, as if she were ordering a ham sandwich instead of talking about the dysfunctional aspects of her family.

"You speak like that dynamic is somehow your fault. I remember Morgan saying you lost your mother at twelve and within a year someone else was taking her place in your family. The adults around you should've seen how difficult that was for you."

She shifted her weight from one foot to the other, leaning her forearms on the railing and clasping her hands together in what seemed like an effort to contain any emotions that might arise.

This definitely wasn't first-date conversation material. He was prying. He knew that. But his need to know her, all about her, made him keep pushing for more.

"I don't think it was at all intentional. I'm an odd duck that my stepmother couldn't really understand. I was withdrawn and had little interest in all the supposedly quintessential girl things Estelle believed a proper little girl should like. It was just easier to leave me and my books be and mold her daughters into perfect socialites from birth."

"You must have been very lonely."

He turned around. With his back facing the open land, he planted his elbows on the balcony railing as he looked down at her. There was still this impassive look he couldn't make heads or tails of.

"I was. But it was a great lesson on how to exist when you're invisible to the rest of the world. Morgan is the only person that's ever seen me and appreciated me for who I am. I shudder to think who I would've become if she hadn't been part of my life to remind me it was okay to like books instead of social climbing as a pastime."

"What does Sanford have to say about all of this?"

Her father was a corporate raider who'd amassed as much money as some of the old money families in Royal.

"Not much," she replied. "It would make Sanford's life much easier if I was the little socialite my little sisters are being raised as. He didn't have all that much tolerance for a sensitive, quiet girl who just wanted to be left alone with her books. Nothing about me makes sense to him. Not my interests, not my career—"

"Wait," Jayden interrupted, facing her again. "You're a doctor. How could he possibly have a problem with that? Sanford seems like a man who likes bragging rights. I can only imagine that having a kid who's a doctor gives him ample things to brag about."

"If I were the right kind of doctor, I imagine he would."

"Right kind?"

She huffed, bringing her eyes to his, accompanied with a weary smile.

"I'm a PsyD, not an MD. So to him, I'm not a real doctor. Even as a psychologist, he probably would've had more respect for me if I'd gotten the almighty PhD. He thinks me getting a PsyD, because my intent was to be a therapist instead of a researcher, is some sort of intellectual failing."

Jayden found himself unconsciously tightening his fists into tight balls. The idea of anyone treating Zanai like that rubbed him raw on the inside. All it took was talking to the woman for five minutes to see how intelligent she was. Her own father calling her otherwise didn't sit right with him.

It didn't seem right, but it wasn't exactly a surprise either. Sanford was big and larger than life. A man who didn't think twice about saying exactly what was on his mind with little care for the people around him. He reminded Jayden of a Black Asa Buchanan, a character on the *One Life to Live* soap opera his grandmother used to watch when Jayden was a kid.

There was also an air about him that made it easy

to believe he wasn't above doing questionable things to get the results he wanted in business and in life.

Jayden's few interactions with the older man had left him cold. The thought of him being that harsh and abrasive with Zanai surprisingly set him on edge.

"You are a brilliant doctor and your father should be proud of your accomplishments. The work you do at the clinic, providing therapy for special-needs kids, that's important, Zanai. Don't ever let anyone tell you different."

She shrugged, waving a dismissive hand in the air before speaking. "It all happened a long time ago and I don't think there's any real way to fix it now. I'm used to it. I don't let it get to me. But never mind all that."

Her smile brightened and the way it lit up her face put him at ease.

"You were saying something about a good time before we got started on all this."

He mirrored her smile, finding it was difficult to stand in her presence and not want to smile and celebrate the light coming from her.

"Not-so-subtle topic change." He wagged a finger at her. "That's okay, I can take a hint. I didn't mean to bring down the mood."

"Don't sweat it. I'm glad I got the chance to talk to you about it. I don't often get that chance to confide such things to anyone else except Morgan. But I'd be lying if I said I didn't want to know more about this good time you mentioned previously."

Recognizing her topic change as a need to cover the exposed parts of her, he willingly switched gears, bringing fun Jayden back to the forefront.

"I will always show you a good time. But I need to make sure we're on the same page here."

"Let me guess." She opened her eyes, staring so intently at him, he could feel her gaze burn through him. "This is only about fun and you don't want any strings?"

That should've been what he was going to say. It had been every other time he'd found himself in this situation with a woman. But somehow, the words coming out of Zanai's mouth didn't sound right to him.

"Don't worry. I'm a big girl. I'm not expecting anything more than fun."

Her delivery wasn't cold. In fact, the warmth of her gaze and the wide smile she was wearing made his blood simmer. But something inside him wished he were the kind of man who would prove Zanai wrong. Because even he could realize that there was something so inviting about this woman that any man would be fortunate to possess.

He was about to say just that when he was reminded that this was his best friend's kid sister's best friend. Things could get messy really quickly if he weren't careful.

He met her gaze, determined to be present in the moment, and decided on a course of action. Better to be careful and let her assume there were no expectations than give her hope for something he wouldn't deliver on. But as he leaned in, pressing his lips to hers, he knew this wouldn't be as simple as *a good time*.

She was hesitant at first. Some men might have interpreted that as inexperience. Perhaps it was. He couldn't recall her being attached to anyone in town. But it didn't read as naïveté, it was more like caution. Like she needed to keep things reserved for some reason unknown to him.

That just wouldn't do. Not since he knew what her skin felt like pressed against his. He needed more, and he would have it.

He wrapped an arm around her waist, pulling her flush against him, before slipping his hand from her face to the base of her neck. He waited a beat for her to get used to him, and when she didn't show signs of discomfort, he tightened his hold and deepened the kiss.

He was perfectly in control until she snaked her arms around his neck, pulling him closer so that there wasn't an inch between them. And when she moaned, like the taste of him against her tongue was the most decadent experience of her life, everything in him wanted to press for more, feel more, taste more of the exquisite creature in his arms.

He pulled away, his rib cage expanding to satiate the air-hunger his lungs were experiencing.

"Exactly how much fun are you willing to have tonight, Zanai?"

There was a flash of something hot and defiant in her eyes that sparked flames in the already hot Texas air. He couldn't help the wicked grin tilting his lips when he recognized it. That thing he'd seen in her gaze at the masquerade ball, the thing that had drawn him to her even when he didn't know her identity.

"As much fun as you're willing to give me."

Hot damn! The woman she kept hidden from the rest of the world just showed up with a hunger in her eyes that rivaled his. This was who he wanted to get to know.

That need to know her had his body hardening in his slacks. Good manners be damned, he didn't care that his arousal was obvious. As far as he was concerned, he wanted her to be fully aware of what she was doing to him.

He slid his hands to her hips, applying just enough pressure to let her know he didn't want her to move, to give her time to get used to the idea of what he hoped they both had in mind.

When she pressed her hips into his, grinding her mound against his cock, he lifted a brow as he looked down into her playful gaze.

"If fun is what the lady wants, that's exactly what she'll get."

Six

Zanai, how the hell did you get here, girl?

If she had the answer to that question there'd be no need for her to keep repeating it over and over in her head.

Her night had started off with a lovely dinner at one of the most popular new restaurants in town, and somehow, she'd gone from a casual dinner and drinks to straddling Jayden Lattimore on his living room couch, topless, with his face currently buried in her cleavage.

As far as nights go, this wasn't a bad thing. But she certainly hadn't expected this. Speaking of the devil with his face in her cleavage, Jayden must have noticed her mind was drifting, because he chose that moment to place a trail of searing kisses against her skin until his plush lips pressed against the curve of her neck. He nipped at the flesh there, applying just the right amount of pressure that her sex clenched and her hips snapped forward searching for the friction she so desperately needed.

"Someone's eager."

Eager didn't quite describe what she was. She wasn't even undressed—not completely anyway—and her body was on fire. She was downright desperate to put out the flames. The only problem was Jayden seemed determined to draw out her desperation as if it turned him on to see her so undone.

If she were more sophisticated, more adept at situations like this, maybe she'd know the right way to tell him to stop teasing her and move this show along. Unfortunately, she wasn't that experienced when it came to matters of seduction. She'd had sex, but this wasn't just about the physical act. This was something altogether different and there was no way she couldn't recognize that.

Subsequently, there was also the added problem that the way Jayden teased and played with her body was so delicious, she didn't want to rush through that either.

His hands pushed her dress up over her hips, exposing heated flesh to the air, making her shiver in delight and anticipation. That anticipation stoked her desire, and by the time he'd slipped gentle fingers beneath her silk panties, she was halfway to climax.

A desperate mewl escaped her lips and she could feel his satisfied smile spreading against her neck. He was enjoying her destruction. Zanai was a proud woman, she almost always avoided situations that made her look like a fool. But as his digits slipped between her slick folds and the pads of his fingers found her clitoris, her pride went running out of the room and all she cared about was the next shock of pleasure that would rip through her.

He didn't disappoint. His fingers played her like an expert musician, coaxing her to the edge of satisfaction but denying her completion, keeping the movement of his composition on tempo until she'd reached the final bars, and her climax peaked with a sharp crescendo that had her calling his name. Caught up in the euphoric harmony he'd written across her flesh, she rode the wave of pleasure until the very last note had come to a strong end.

As she came back to herself, thoughts of how desperate and needy she must look began to creep into her mind. She closed her eyes, trying to shrink back and find some way out of this awkward predicament she'd found herself in.

"No, don't do that."

His words pulled her gaze to his. She didn't have the chance to speak, not that she could if she wanted to. She was completely mesmerized by the heated spark in his eyes.

"You have nothing to be ashamed of. Everything about this moment is beautiful, including the way you just lost yourself in my arms."

Zanai fought the audible sigh she could feel gathering in her chest. Could this man be any more sexy? If there was a way he could be, she was certain Jayden Lattimore would find it. As if the soothing way he'd coaxed her through her orgasm wasn't enough to spark her arousal all over again, his reassuring words made sizzling heat burn through the layers of her skin.

Without thought, she pressed her lips to his as she slid her hands down his chest until her fingers reached the belt buckle at his waist. She was about to pull it free of its clasp when his hands stilled hers.

"Don't you want me to—"

"I most certainly do." His breathing was labored, as if the very act of speaking hurt. "But not tonight. I meant what I said about coaxing your inner queen out into the open. I'm going to treat you like a queen until you finally accept that's who and what you are."

She'd heard and understood every word he'd spoken, and somehow, she still couldn't believe his intention. Outside of Morgan, none of the elite of Royal had paid her this much attention before, least of all her own family.

"Why is this so important to you, Jayden? What

do you get out of me embracing my 'inner queen,' as you call her?"

He snaked his hand around the base of her neck and pulled her forward, slamming his mouth against hers and drinking from her very essence.

"Oh, the answer is so very easy, Doctor. This is a selfish ploy. For my own self-interest, I want you to be everything you felt free enough to be at that masquerade ball for one simple reason. The fierce creature I danced with is the sexiest woman I've ever seen, and I want her back so I can do all the wicked things to her that my lecherous mind thought up while we were on that dance floor."

Her pulse raced as fire spread throughout her body. She was being utterly undone by this man's words, and she didn't care one bit. The warning bells were clanging in her head that letting Jayden in was dangerous. She'd carefully orchestrated everything in her life to have the things she wanted most: complete her undergrad and graduate work, pass her state licensure exams, build a mental health clinic for those that didn't traditionally have access. That's it and that's all.

There was only one problem now—Jayden was included in that very specific list of things she had to do. And more than anything, she knew that fiery desire he seemed to stoke in her meant at some point, all of this would fall apart.

Seven

Zanai tensed as she heard her father's and step-mother's voices float into the hallway. She was usually gone by this hour of the day, but a late night with one Jayden Lattimore last night and she'd snoozed her alarm one too many times.

As a twenty-eight-year-old professional, there was no reason she should have to skulk out of her house to avoid her disapproving parents. But when your father was Sanford James and he seemed to disapprove of everything about you, it was much easier just to leave before he awoke.

Recognizing she couldn't stand in the middle of the hallway all day, she smoothed one hand down the front of her button-down shirt as the other tightened around her tote bag. With her shoulders pulled back, she continued her journey down the hall to her intended target of the front door.

She'd made it one step beyond the dining room's entryway when she heard her father belt out her name.

Zanai paused midstep, part of her determined to pretend she hadn't heard Sanford.

"I know you heard me, gal."

And he knew she hated to be called that too. Sanford was born and bred in Brooklyn, just like Zanai. His use of the word *gal* when directed at her annoyed the hell out of her because it was always meant to diminish her, to put her in her place. She knew it and so did her father.

She turned on her heel, walking through the dining room entryway to find Sanford and his wife, Estelle, seated at the grand table at the center of the room.

"Father, Estelle, good morning."

Neither of them looked up from their plates nor immediately spoke. And like always, the silence made her want to shift from one foot to the other in discomfort.

"You got in rather late last night," her father commented as he used his utensils to cut through the food on his plate.

Sanford James didn't ask questions. He made statements in a way that compelled the people around him to offer up explanations. This time was no different.

"I was working." She kept her voice neutral, hoping her father wouldn't pick up the scent of blood in the water. "The clinic is in need of funding, so I had to schmooze a potential benefactor last night."

Sanford slowly raised his eyes to hers, his cold, hard glare piercing through her like a dagger.

"You and that damn clinic. You are Sanford James's daughter. You asking for handouts from these old money snobs in Royal makes me look bad, Zanai."

She shook her head as frustration bubbled up inside of her.

"Father, we've been over this. Me being a therapist at the clinic doesn't have any bearing on you or your business."

"That's where you're wrong," Estelle interjected. "It's a clinic for the indigent. For a man of your father's status, what does it say if his daughter is dealing with the dregs of society every day?"

Zanai's sharp gaze slammed into Estelle's. Usually, she did her best to stay out of the woman's way. Incurring her stepmother's wrath always meant triggering her father's as well. This morning, however, she couldn't seem to get a proper hold on her anger as it twisted inside her.

"Being poor isn't a crime, Estelle. I work with innocent kids who are neurodivergent, not criminals.

They shouldn't be punished simply because they weren't born into privilege or didn't marry into it."

Estelle blinked at her, the shock on her face clear and unmistakable. Zanai was filled with a brief swell of pride before she realized what she'd done.

"Don't talk to your mother like that, Zanai."

"She's not my mother. She's your wife." The words slipped out before she could stop them and she had to wonder what the hell was going on with her today.

A few hours in Jayden's presence was already screwing with her head and causing her to put herself on her father's radar, which was never a good thing.

"Don't speak about Estelle that way. She's sacrificed too much to take care of you."

That wasn't exactly how Zanai remembered it. The only time Estelle paid attention to Zanai was while she was trying to become Mrs. Sanford James. The moment the deal was sealed, she ignored Zanai like a forgotten toy shoved in a basement storage room.

"Father, I don't wish to fight with either of you. All I ask is that you respect my choice to work at the clinic. It's where I'm most needed."

"Where you're most needed is where I say you're needed." Sanford's voice filled the large room, nearly making everything from the chandelier crystals to the silverware shake. "You need to be using any talent you have to help me get into the good graces of these bigwigs around here. If you're not doing that, you're a waste."

She'd heard these words before too many times to be shocked by the amount of cruelty they were dipped in. But even though she expected them, it didn't stop them from hurting her either.

She swallowed, any fight she had in her disappearing into the ether. She simply nodded her head and said, "Yes, father," in a quiet voice before turning toward the door and slithering out of the house in shame.

She sat in her car, wishing beyond reason that she possessed the qualities Jayden had insisted she had. If there were ever a time for her inner queen to show up, it was now. But sadly, her absence made Zanai fear what she'd always suspected—that queen was a figment of Jayden's imagination and hers.

"Hey, you. How's your day going?"

Zanai smiled as Jayden's easy baritone drifted through her phone. "It was a little rocky this morning, but it's getting exponentially better at the moment."

"I'm glad to hear that. I'm going to choose to believe I'm solely responsible for making it better."

He didn't have to try to take credit for it. He was the reason, plain and simple. After her exchange with her father and Estelle that morning, her focus was off and she couldn't seem to get half of what she needed to done. But just hearing his voice pushed back the dark clouds lingering over her all day.

"You are so full of confidence, aren't you?"

"Of course I am," he quipped. "I'm Ben and Barbara Lattimore's baby boy. That's all the reason I need to be confident."

"You're a mess," she playfully mocked him. "You know that, right?"

His amusement filled the line, washing over her like a warm blanket that kept out the cold. "I've been called worse."

She was sure he had. But by his easygoing demeanor, she couldn't imagine it had ever bothered him.

"What can I do for you, Mr. Lattimore?"

"Direct and straight to the point, good Doctor. I like that."

She liked being able to be this way with him. But she wouldn't admit it. Not because she didn't want him to know she enjoyed the effect he had on her, that wasn't it. She didn't want him to know just how pitiful she was when it came to being direct with someone like her father.

"If you're getting off work at a reasonable time today, how would you feel about having dinner with me at the ranch?"

"You mean, with your family?"

She could feel a slight flash of panic rising in her. From everything she'd ever known about the Lattimores, they were a lovely group of people. But after dealing with her own family this morning, having to take on someone else's, no matter how nice they were, wasn't on her agenda.

"Don't sound so nervous. It's not that kind of dinner. If you wanna eat with the Lattimore clan, I can arrange that. But I was thinking something more private. If you can get here in the next hour, we'll have enough daylight left to eat outside."

She could feel the nervous tension slipping away as he described his plans. Oh, there was still tension, but a different kind that began to grow at the thought of spending alone time in a quiet place with one Jayden Lattimore.

"I just saw my last patient. Let me go home to shower and change and I can meet you in an hour."

He moaned softly through the line and she couldn't help but giggle like a schoolgirl. "I promise you won't regret it."

His reassurance wasn't necessary. She knew beyond a shadow of a doubt that she would enjoy every minute of her time spent with him.

Eight

The Lattimore ranch was a huge display of sprawling greenery for as far as the eye could see. She drove slowly up the path taking in the colorful garden and landscaping design. It was lush and lavish, not unlike the property she lived on. But where Sanford and Estelle's design style was ostentatious and cold like a museum, the Lattimores' home, even from the outside, looked welcoming and lived-in, like they actually took time to enjoy their wealth.

She pulled up slowly to the front of the house, cutting the engine and praying that whatever Jayden had in mind tonight, she wouldn't goof it up by being her usual awkward self.

She was still reeling from their time together in his apartment. Everything in her had wanted to continue. Why wouldn't she? She'd never felt so desired in all her life.

Zanai's sex life, for lack of a better word, sucked. She'd dated a couple of men throughout college and graduate school, but her time with them hadn't felt anything like the heated touches she'd shared with Jayden.

Everything about him, from the way his dark brown eyes made her feel seen in places she hadn't realized she possessed, to the way she burned when his skin met hers, was electric and addictive.

A few moments in his arms and she couldn't stop herself from thinking about him. And that was a problem. If his touch was this powerful and they hadn't actually had sex yet, how far gone would she be when she actually knew what having his body joined with hers felt like?

The certainty in that thought didn't slip her notice. She wholeheartedly intended that they would cross that threshold of intimacy. However, wanting it this badly worried her. If she was this needy already, how much more control would she lose when Jayden finally gave her what she wanted?

He's not the "forever" kind of guy, Zanai. This is just fun to him. You'd do well to remember that before you get your heart broken.

As if on cue, the object of her musings stepped

through the grand doors, making his way out onto the circular driveway and walking over to the driver's side of her car.

"Hey, beautiful." His face was all aglow with easy charm, lulling her into what felt like a powerful trance.

How many women had he given that lazy smile to? How many more would know that simple pleasure after her?

Unwilling to entertain the idea for fear of ruining their time together, she focused instead on him, turning her face to the side and giving him a wide grin.

"I bet you say that to all the girls you invite here."

He leaned down into her window, giving her a quick peck on the lips. "That would be a bet you'd lose. I've never brought anyone to the main house."

While she sat stunned, trying to figure out if he was just feeding her a line or telling the truth, he squeezed her hand, giving her that roguish grin again that seemed to warm all the cold, dark places inside her.

He has to practice that. There's no way his smile became that devastating without years and years of practice.

"The main house is currently filled with my siblings, who will take any chance they have to make me look bad in front of company. So we're gonna have to eat out on the deck of my cottage. Follow me." She watched him get in his pickup truck, and she pulled out behind him on the gravel road leading away from the main house.

After a short drive, they arrived at their destination. This time she took in more details. The cottage was a mix of modern and rugged. Wooded cabin-like walls, a mounted flat-screen television, a large sectional in the middle of the room and decorative artwork throughout. The open floor plan was inviting and stylish.

"The main house appears huge on the outside. Aren't there enough rooms for all of you to remain in the house?"

With their hands entwined, he ran his thumb over her skin, making it hard for her to focus on anything but the places where their flesh touched.

"We do each have rooms in the house. But having my cottage means I get to be selfish and not share you with anyone else. Come on, I haven't shown you my favorite part yet: the back deck."

She followed his lead to a large square-shaped deck. The wood was painted a reddish brown with plush lounge sofas in three of its four corners filled with pillows in various shades of brown. The last corner housed a large grill that looked as if it belonged in a restaurant rather than someone's backyard.

"I take it someone enjoys their barbecue?"

Pride beamed on his face. Even in the dimly lit backyard, she could still see excitement glowing in his eyes.

"I'm a Texan, darlin'. Grilled meat over an open flame is kinda what we do."

She nodded, pointing in the direction of the grill. "You any good with that thing? Or is it just for decoration?"

His jaw dropped and he placed a hand over his heart. "You wound me with your words, woman. I come from a long line of pit masters. I might be useless in a kitchen, but I'm a king on a grill."

"You got proof or should I just accept your word for it?"

"See, those sound like fighting words to me. She's already heated. You go take a seat and I'll grab everything I need from inside."

Amusement flowed through her as she appreciated this playful side of him. "Someone's confident in his skills."

He shrugged. "Because I'm amazing at everything I do." He stole a quick kiss and disappeared back into the house, leaving her grinning wide despite her earlier reminder to play it cool. Jayden was a player, admittedly so. But that didn't mean she had to let herself get played. *Keep it light and fun, Zanai. That's the only way you walk out of here unscathed.*

"On everything I love, that was the best barbecue I've ever had."

"I told you my skills were unmatched."

He watched her lean back in her seat with her

hand on her stomach. "I can't remember the last time I've been this full. You truly are skilled, Jayden."

"I know."

Her shoulders shook with laughter and it warmed him that she could tell he was joking. Sometimes his confident, yet easygoing manner came off as arrogance. But the way amusement beamed in her eyes, he could tell she understood this was just him being him.

"I don't think I can move. I'm stuffed."

"Good, that means I've done my job as grill master tonight. Rest up a few minutes while I clear the table."

She attempted to stand, presumably to help him with their used dishes.

"Nope," he admonished. "You're a guest, and it would be bad manners for you to lift a finger. I live to serve you, my queen."

He worked as quickly as possible to clear the table, rinse the dishes and get the dishwasher situated. He didn't want to spend one moment longer than necessary away from Zanai, but dried barbecue sauce on flatware was not fun and Josie, the family housekeeper, would have his head if she found a speck of dried food on those dishes.

When the machine was humming, he grabbed two longnecks from the fridge and headed back to the deck, to Zanai.

He couldn't remember exactly when spending

even a few moments away from her became such a hardship. Thinking back, he couldn't pinpoint a specific moment, he only knew that when he was away from her for any amount of time, he felt antsy, unsettled.

The idea of being this attached to any woman didn't sit well with him, not usually anyway. But Zanai James had somehow changed things for him. He wasn't ready to admit this was anything more than fun. Yet, he wasn't foolish enough to ignore how tightly wound around her finger he was becoming either.

He found her standing, looking beyond the deck at his gazebo, which had a firepit in the center of it.

"It's cool enough to sit by the fire tonight if you'd like."

At the sound of his voice, she drew her gaze back to his.

"I don't want you to go through all that trouble if you hadn't already planned to do so."

"I told you, I live to serve you. It's really no trouble at all."

He took her hand, helping her down the few steps from the deck before leading her to the gazebo.

He handed her the beers in his hand and set about starting the fire in front of them. In short order, the small flames began to warm the cool night air and he took his seat next to her, grabbing the beer she offered to him as he relaxed into the cushions.

"So, how was work today?"

Incongruence weighed heavily on her delicate features and he wondered if he'd touched a sore spot by bringing up her work.

"You don't have to do that."

"Do what?"

"Ask about my work like it's interesting."

"I'm confused," he replied. "Why wouldn't I find what you do interesting? You've practically built that clinic from the ground up and given kids who need good mental health care a means to have it even if their families can't afford it."

She took a long sip of her beer and he surmised it had more to do with avoidance than thirst.

"I do. But most people aren't interested in talking about the mental health profession as light, after-dinner conversation."

He threaded his fingers through hers, resting their entwined hands on his thigh.

"Zanai, you could've chosen to treat rich socialites who treat therapy like a fashion accessory. Instead, you treat a very specific population that's often overlooked. No to mention, for all the wealth in Royal, there are still parts that struggle with poverty. Don't think I haven't noticed that you started your clinic in an area that's 90 percent Black and Brown people, where poverty hits hardest in these parts."

He wasn't exaggerating. The clinic was on the edge of town, physically removed from the pretty parts of Royal that thrived at the town's center. Setting up shop there had to have been an intentional choice.

"It's not just that," he continued. "You know the stigma in Black communities when it comes to mental health care. So many of us suffer undiagnosed and untreated mental health conditions and we never seek help because we falsely believe therapy isn't for Black folks."

The widening of her eyes told him he'd hit the nail on the head again.

"That was the very reason I'd gone into the mental health profession. I'd seen the effects firsthand of the disproportionate amount of care in our communities.

"Some of it is because of lack of access. But there is a large portion who, even though access isn't an issue, they won't seek help for fear of the stigma in the community."

He leaned down, pressing his lips to hers, feeling the warm buzz of his beer being chased with the intoxicating taste of her. He gentled the kiss, pulling away from her before giving her still-entangled hand a squeeze.

"You are obviously dedicated to your work and to this issue. How could I not be interested in hearing about the work you do when it's so important, and obviously so important to you?"

There was something distant in her eyes, a fog covering up the bright light he'd witnessed all night.

She shifted in her seat, pulling her hand out of his and picking away at the label on the beer bottle.

"It's important to me because of all the reasons you listed. But it's also important to me because my mother died of an undiagnosed mental health condition."

Her voice, the statement, it was all detached, as if this was strictly a clinical matter that wasn't personally linked to her. She could've been talking about any of her patients from the cool tone of her voice.

It didn't matter to him how distant she sounded. Wherever she was taking this conversation, everything in him screamed at him to give her support.

So he did.

He leaned over, wrapping his arm around her shoulders and tugging her into his side.

"My mother was so beautiful, giving and kind. She truly loved life. But being in an unhealthy relationship with my father eventually took its toll on her.

"She loved me, and was the best mother to me. But looking back on it with a clinical eye, I can pinpoint the many depressive episodes she had. My aunt begged her to get help and when she wouldn't, she begged my father to get her help. Unfortunately, he was too busy trying to build his empire. He thought having a wife in treatment would embarrass him and negatively impact his business."

Tiny tremors began to course through him and he

couldn't tell if the vibrations were coming from him or Zanai. Either way, he tightened his hold on her, trying his best to let her know he was there for her.

"When I was eleven, she was in a car accident where she sustained back injuries. The injuries weren't severe enough to be debilitating, but her doctors gave her pain pills to ease her discomfort."

She shifted again, somehow burrowing herself deeper into his side. He rubbed his hand up and down her arm, trying to soothe her.

"She became addicted to those pills. And because they were prescribed, they didn't have the negative association illicit drugs have, so no one recognized there was a problem. Yeah, she said she was using them for her back pain. But looking back I can see she was just self-medicating to get through her depressive episodes.

"A year later, she died of what was documented as an accidental overdose of prescribed medication. But the days leading up to her death make part of me feel that maybe it wasn't so accidental after all. Not the way she kept reminding me that no matter what, she loved me. That her choices were her own flaws and not mine."

"You think she committed suicide?"

"The truth?" she huffed, as if finally unburdened by a heavy weight. "I don't know. I'll never know. Because her death was filed as accidental, her insurance company paid out three million dollars. Two-thirds of it went to me in a trust that paid for my education and helped me start the clinic, leaving the remaining million to Sanford. He used that money to start his business. He built his empire on the death of his wife."

Jayden's interactions with Sanford James were very limited. Sanford was a corporate raider. Thankfully that meant there wasn't much crossover between their respective areas of business. However, what little he did know of the man, Jayden had never liked.

After listening to Zanai, it was hard to find any redeeming qualities about him.

"Losing my mom the way I did left me with so many unanswered questions about my own mental health. So when girls my age were learning to be social butterflies, I was reading everything I could on depression and other mental health conditions."

"Because you wanted to make sure you weren't suffering the same symptoms yourself."

Silence hung between them. It wasn't awkward where either of them felt they had to fill the space. Instead, it was full of understanding, of compassion, of need.

As his arm tightened around her shoulders, pulling her into his frame, she wrapped her arms around his waist as if he were an anchor. And as much as part of him screamed at the intimacy of it all, he was glad she somehow instinctively knew she could lean on him.

"I'm sorry." She whispered those words while her face was pressed against his chest, and although quietly spoken, they seeped through his chest wall and somehow managed to wrap themselves around his heart.

"What on earth are you apologizing for?"

"Ruining the evening. You asked me how was work, and I go on and on about my dysfunctional family. I guess you can see now why this dating thing doesn't really work for me. I don't know how to do any of this."

"Zanai, look at me."

She complied, sitting up, bringing her soulful gaze to his. There was pain there. It wasn't fresh as if it was an open wound, but chronic, like she'd been carrying it for so long and now she was weary.

"Don't ever apologize for who you are. There's nothing wrong with you, then or now. Socialites are overrated. And if I cared about being with one, I certainly wouldn't be here with you. It's you I want, and nothing you can tell me about your past is going to change that fact."

She watched him, seemingly scanning every inch of his face. She was obviously trying to make sense of him, attempting to figure out why he wanted to be there so desperately. He could see her questions filling her dark brown eyes and it angered part of him that people had treated her so poorly, her baseline expectation was that no one wanted to be around her.

"You have to say that. Otherwise, your little social experiment won't work."

Something hot and angry sliced through him, causing him to pull out of her embrace. He could see by her pinched brow that he'd caught of her off guard. He didn't care.

"Zanai, if this were a social experiment, I'd be trying to make you into something you're not."

She shrugged as uncertainty danced in her eyes. "Isn't that what you're trying to do?"

He shook his head. He'd meant it when he'd told his sister he wasn't trying to change Zanai. But apparently, he needed to explain himself more if both women, women that he respected, seemed to think so.

"I'm not trying to make you into something you're not, Zanai. I'm trying to bring out what I already see there. The strength, the regal beauty, the fortitude to be an agent of change and provide help and a voice to the voiceless. That's who I see you as, Zanai. The only thing that's different about me is that I want to honor and celebrate who you are. I want to bask in your light. So please, stop comparing me to all the foolish people that have worked so hard to dim it."

Her expression was unreadable, and he worried that if he let her wallow in her thoughts, she'd withdraw from him again.

A kiss was the only answer. If she wouldn't listen to his words, then maybe he could convey his feelings through touch.

He'd intended the kiss to be patient and reassuring. It didn't quite work out that way, however. As soon as his lips pressed against the soft cushion of her mouth, gentle went out of the window and need moved right in, putting its feet up and getting comfortable.

The taste of her, like the barbecue they'd eaten, was sweet and tangy, with just the right hint of spice that slowly burned through his system catching him unaware before exploding into flames.

He tore his mouth away from hers in an effort to regain his composure. He was on fire and if he didn't get control of this situation, he'd strip her right here and have her in the gazebo. But he wanted more for her, more from her too.

Her brown skin was gleaming with a reddish glow as she attempted to catch her breath and his ego did a little happy dance because she was just as undone as he was.

"You are really something, Mr. Lattimore."

"I am," he replied. "Now, if I could only get my siblings to acknowledge that, all would be right in my world."

A conspiratorial grin spread on her face as she leaned into him. "Well, they won't hear that from me. I think if too many people acknowledge that, your ego might not be able to fit comfortably in another room."

He couldn't argue with her. Not with the way her smile delighted him and her touch made him burn. Everything about Zanai James did it for him, and he knew part of that was knowing that he absolutely did it for her as well.

Nine

"Okay, spill it. I need all the details."

Zanai looked up from the fashion magazine she'd plucked from a nearby table, squinting as she tried to figure out the meaning behind her best friend's outburst.

"I'm not sure I know what you mean."

"You've been out with Jayden Lattimore almost every night this week and you haven't called me once to tell me how it's going."

Understanding dawned, causing Zanai to nod in acknowledgement of her friend's claims.

"It's been great."

Morgan walked from behind the counter and

flipped the sign on the door to the "Closed" position before she came to sit down next to Zanai in the empty store.

"That's it? You're dating the most eligible bachelor in Royal and all you have to say is 'It's been great'?"

"It *has* been great." Zanai shrugged. "Jayden is the perfect gentleman, a perfect Prince Charming."

"And that's why you're being all nonchalant about this? You don't believe he's real, do you?"

Zanai sighed loudly as she closed the magazine in her hands and tossed it back on the nearby table.

"He's a charmer. He knows how to make people feel good around him, especially women. None of this is real."

Her mind drifted back to the evening she'd had dinner at his cottage a few nights ago. That night had certainly felt real. From the good food and conversation, to the profound way he'd supported her while she revealed the circumstances of her mother's death, every second of it had felt real and tangible. And it was terrifying her.

Morgan simply shook her head and threw up her hands in frustration. "You can't be serious. I know Jayden, he does not do repeats. He certainly doesn't bring women to the Lattimore ranch. Yet, he's done both those things for you. Why can't you believe this is real?"

Because if it's real, then it can go away, then it can hurt me.

She already knew what it was like to lose someone special in her life. She didn't want to add Jayden to the mix. So if she planned to protect herself, and she did, she couldn't take any of Jayden's advances seriously.

"I wouldn't categorize Jayden as a player. But he's not looking for anything serious. He's been very clear about that. We're just enjoying each other's company for the time being. There's no need to complicate this more by trying to figure out if the man is sincere in his pursuit of me."

Morgan sat there with her mouth open and eyes wide. Her disbelief was evident and warranted. But Zanai could never let her know that, not when it meant Zanai would inevitably cry all over Morgan's shoulders when Jayden finally was through playing with his new toy.

"You're unbelievable. Only you could get the man every other single woman in this town is clamoring for, and you're acting like he's a cheap wine cooler when he's really a fifty-year-old perfectly aged scotch. How can you be so detached?"

"I'm simply not letting my emotions get the better of me. That's not the same thing as being detached, Morgan."

A flash of light illuminated Morgan's eyes. "So you do have feelings for him?"

Of course she did. Especially after that night in his gazebo.

It had felt so wonderful to, even for a moment, lay her burdens in his arms. However, when she'd gone home alone that night, she'd ached for him so terribly, she'd hardly slept.

That need for him, the strong, addictive thing that was growing in her belly, demanding she satisfy this hunger, that was the thing she had to fight against. Because becoming dependent on a man who could never love her like she needed to be was a fool's game. She'd watched it destroy her mother, and she vowed it would never be her.

Not now, not ever.

Jayden walked into the Royal Diner aching for a burger and fries. Yes, he could've made that at home, or asked the family chef to make it for him up at the big house. But he'd needed to get out of his house and talk to someone about everything that was happening with Zanai.

He scanned the restaurant, relaxing his shoulders as a sense of relief descended upon him once he glimpsed his friend Ryan at a booth in the back of the eatery.

In a few strides, he was sitting down next to a man he'd known for a lot of years. Ryan's blond hair and blue eyes belied the grumpy bastard that he truly was. Right now, though, it was that blunt, unaffected persona that Jayden needed the most.

"Hey, man, thanks for meeting me." Jayden's words were met with a grunt and a nod. More amused than offended, Jayden smirked at his friend's response.

Their server came and placed fresh cups of coffee in front of them and quickly took their orders. Once alone, though, Ryan glanced up at Jayden with just enough impatience or intolerance, at this point he really couldn't tell which, swimming in his gaze.

"You wanna get to the point why I'm out here in downtown Royal instead being back on my ranch?"

"Same old Ryan," Jayden muttered to himself. "I needed some advice."

"And you're coming to me?" Ryan's query made Jayden snicker. "You must be desperate. What about Vic?"

Jayden shook his head at the mention of his best friend's name.

"Not for this. Not yet anyway. Vic and Morgan are thick as thieves, and if I tell Vic what's going on, I have no doubt it will spread like wildfires on dry land."

Ryan sat up then, realizing how serious this situation must be.

"I've been hanging out with Zanai James for the last bit."

"Is hanging out a euphemism for dating or sex? I need the clarification."

Jayden's wry laugh didn't put Ryan off. The man still stared at him waiting for an answer.

"Dating," Jayden replied, "and some serious petting. We haven't gotten to the sex part yet, although I presume that's coming soon."

Ryan waved his hand in a "hurry up and spill it already" fashion to get Jayden to get on with the full story.

"Things are getting a bit hot and heavy, and I wanted to talk about the pros and cons of that. You think you can spare a moment for me?"

Something softened in Ryan's face, as if he was somehow less annoyed with Jayden's need to talk. He sighed deeply and sat back in his chair.

"What's going on, man?"

"I… This woman."

"If you're dating her, I assume that's a good thing, right?"

Jayden wasn't so sure about that. He didn't do serious relationships, ever.

"It feels good."

Ryan looked at him, nodding as if he was processing some sort of calculation in his head.

"And that's the problem, right? It feels good and you don't know what to do with that."

"Well…yeah," he hedged. Briefly taken aback by Ryan's uncharacteristic display of emotional awareness, Jayden reached for the cup of coffee their server had poured before she took their orders to the kitchen. "That's oddly perceptive of you."

"Choosing not to deal with people's nonsense is not the same thing as being unaware, Jay."

Jayden leaned back in his chair, his jaw dropping open ever so slightly with disbelief mixed with a bit of suspicion.

"Fine." Ryan threw up his hands before letting them lightly hit the table in front of them. "We both know I'm not that enlightened. Let's just say, I did something really stupid lately that's got me thinking about things I wouldn't normally waste a thought on."

Jayden couldn't disguise his amusement at his friend's response. This sounded more like the Ryan he knew, so stuck on doing things his way he rarely recognized anything or anyone around him.

"Care to elaborate?"

Ryan shot him a sharp glance that Jayden found more comical than he should have. It possibly made him a bad friend, but it made him feel better that he wasn't the only person walking around rethinking everything he thought he knew about himself.

"No, I don't." Ryan crossed his arms, an attempt to conceal how affected he was by whatever was going on with him. "Truth is, I couldn't if I wanted to. I'm out of my depth here, so I can't possibly give you any advice on how to handle your own situation."

Ryan's response hung in the air while their server returned with their food. Once they were alone again, Jayden looked up at his friend with a bit of commiseration in his chest.

"I don't know exactly what's going on, but if you need to talk about it, you know I'm here, right?"

Ryan shrugged a dismissive shoulder, but Jayden could see the appreciation swimming in his eyes.

"Thanks, man," he grumbled around a forkful of food as if he didn't really want Jayden to hear him. "'Preciate it. Just wish I could be some help to you."

So did Jayden, but it seemed he was going to have to figure this one out on his own. Unfortunately, he had the feeling that he'd better come up with a plan soon enough. He'd started out this thing hoping to have an impact on Zanai. But he'd never accounted for the fact that just being in her presence could somehow alter who he was too.

Out of any useful ideas, he picked up his fork and tucked into his food. No sense in dwelling on something when he hadn't a clue what he was dealing with in the first place.

Sure, Jayden. Ignore it, pretend that there's no problem at all. That always works, right?

"Lunch has arrived, m'lady."

She looked up from the bag of takeout Jayden had placed in her hand and smiled. Her day had started with a mountain of work and very little time to do much more than jump from one patient's session to the next. Days like this meant she'd have to cancel the prior lunch plans she'd made with Jayden.

Refusing to let her cancel, he'd shown up to the clinic with takeout from the diner in hand. He'd given her the food, kissed her on her cheek and said for her to call him if she got a moment later.

So overwhelmed by his kindness, she'd barely recognized his intention was to leave.

"You're not going to eat with me?"

"You're busy, and I'm not here to be a distraction. I just wanted to make sure you had enough fuel to keep doing what you do."

She fought to keep her jaw from dropping. A grown, self-possessed man who didn't need to be the center of a woman's world. Was she dreaming?

He'd just turned toward the door to leave when he looked back, tossing a wink over his shoulder and disarming her even more than his impromptu lunch delivery.

"By the way, are you free this weekend?"

"Yeah. You wanna do something?"

"Possibly. I'll give you the details when we talk on your way home."

Exciting anticipation whirled in her belly. So much so, she wasn't even going to allow her head to tell her she shouldn't be excited by such small things. All this man had done was bring her takeout and promise to talk to her on her ride home. But the more time she spent with Jayden, the more she realized it was the small things that she liked so much about him.

"You up for a trip tomorrow?"

If she weren't driving, she would've glanced down at her phone to make sure she'd heard him correctly.

"A trip where?"

Since they'd started whatever this was they were doing, Jayden always called her so he could keep her company on her trips home.

The clinic was only about thirty minutes from her house, hardly enough time to feel lonely on the road or get into any real danger. But she was still grateful to hear his voice nonetheless.

"To New York. We could catch a play, see the sights and then have a nice dinner."

Her brows knit together before a cautious smile spread across her lips. "Jayden Lattimore, is this your attempt to wine and dine me?"

"It most certainly is. After a day like today, you deserve it. The question is, are you going to let me?"

Her smiled widened. "Most definitely."

"Great." The excited lilt in his voice made warmth spread through her. Why did such simple things endear this man to her more and more?

"Meet me at my house first thing in the morning and we'll head out."

"Will do." She nodded and smiled to herself with

the hope of something decadent dancing in her head. Her expectations were high, just as he'd intended if she were gauging his voice correctly. The fun part was going to be spending an entire day watching him deliver on everything his words promised.

The truth was, he already had surpassed her expectations with the simple gesture of bringing her lunch when she was too busy to get it herself earlier today. This was just dessert on top of an already decadent meal.

As they continued their call, finalizing their plans, she wondered how on earth she'd ever managed to live without such treatment all her life.

Ten

"You're from New York, I can't believe you're so unfamiliar with your surroundings."

Zanai laughed as they milled through the throng of people in Times Square, heading back to their nearby hotel.

"I'm from Brooklyn. Totally different place from what you call New York."

"What I call New York? I'm not sure what you mean by that."

She slid her hand down from his forearm until her fingers were intertwining with his. "Tourists call this 'New York' or 'New York City.' Those of us who were born and raised here call it 'Manhattan.' And when you're from Brooklyn, for the most part, you only go into Manhattan when you have to. There are just too many folks out here, most of them tourists like you."

With their fingers interlaced, he squeezed her digits lightly, before offering her a smile. "So Brooklyn is like the Wild West of New York."

She shook her head. "No, it's actually to the east of Manhattan." Her matter-of-fact tone had the desired effect, tugging a generous grin onto Jayden's face. "Manhattan is beautiful, but it can be so noisy and chaotic, dealing with that on a daily basis can be a little tiresome. Sometimes you just want a much more relaxed vibe."

He nodded, stepping aside so she could walk through the revolving doors first.

He waited until they'd made their way on the elevator and then stepped off at their designated floor before continuing the conversation.

"I can see how the city could be a bit much on a consistent basis. Sometimes you just need to relax and breathe."

He pulled out his keycard, tapping it against the lock and waiting for the requisite light to flash green before he turned the knob and held the door open for her.

Forever the gentleman, he stepped aside and let her walk in first.

Almost immediately, she noticed something was

off. The lights were dimmed with an artificial candlelit glow covering the entire sitting area.

In the center of the room was a small square table draped in a velvet cloth, adorned with a chrome champagne bucket and elegant crystal drinkware.

"What have you done, Jayden?"

When she turned around, he was standing there in a relaxed stance, his feet spread wide with his hands shoved in the pockets of his trousers, looking as smooth and unaffected as he could be.

"You work hard, and from what I can tell, you hardly take any time to indulge yourself. I just wanted to make sure you took a few moments to do so while we were here. Not to mention, after spending most of my time with cows and horses and their respective aromas, it's nice for me to enjoy fancy digs too."

There was something about the way he said the world indulge that made her shiver with expectation. It wasn't overtly sexual in nature, but there were some heated undertones there that alluded to the potential this night could hold.

She looked into his eyes, his gaze so powerful, she could feel herself falling endlessly the more she stared at him.

She tore her eyes away from his to give herself a brief reprieve, and that's when she saw them. Rose petals scattered across the floor leading from the table to his room in their suite.

"You really went all out, huh?"

He stepped closer. "I told you, a queen deserves the very best. Let's eat, and then we can see how the rest of the night unfolds."

The weight of his focused gaze on her was too much to bear. It wasn't just on her, but somehow burrowing through her, seeing the absolute truth of who she was: a scared and lonely woman who'd built walls around herself to keep the world out.

"So, what are we celebrating?" She walked over to the table, picking up the glasses and nodding toward the chilling bottle in the bucket. He continued to watch her for a moment before he stepped forward and made quick work of popping the cork.

He dropped his gaze for the few seconds it took him to fill their glasses, and once the bottle was settled back in its icy nest, he was right back to watching her.

"As always, we're celebrating you." He gently touched his glass to hers before taking a measured sip of the bubbly liquid and setting his glass down on the table.

"Zanai, you don't have to be nervous. I set all of this up because I thought you'd like it. But nothing I've done means I expect you to sleep with me. Whether we spend the night eating snacks and watching TV or pleasuring each other until we're both too tired to move, it's your choice."

He tilted his head as if he were calculating something. Whatever conclusion he'd come to, his expression softened a bit. The need that seemed to be running just beneath the surface of his skin was still there, providing his dark complexion with a reddish tint that made her have to fight to keep her hands to herself.

He extended his hand until his palm was caressing her cheek, resulting in a decadent sigh that spilled from her lips involuntarily.

"What's going on in that beautiful mind of yours?"

She pressed her face into the warmth of his hand, his touch instantly soothing the nerves in her belly. If she could just stay like this and not think this to death, she'd probably have the best time of her life.

"I've enjoyed our time together. And by the way I so easily go up in flames every time you touch me, I hope you know, wanting this is not the problem."

"Then what is? Because I definitely see hesitation in your eyes. As much as I want you, I won't take what isn't freely given. There's no joy in that for me. So what's holding you back?"

She swallowed, closing her eyes briefly to gather her strength before locking her gaze with his.

"This is going to sound so immature and unsophisticated, but I'm just afraid this will change things between us."

She could see his brow pulling into a tight V as

he continued to search her face for answers, silently prodding her to continue.

"You call me a queen, Jayden." She took a sip of her champagne, hoping it would provide her with just a touch of some of that liquid courage she'd heard so much about. "But the truth is, the time we've spent together has been the only instance in my life where I've felt like one."

"And you think once I get what I want, all that goes away?"

Said out loud, his assumption sounded ridiculous, but that didn't make it any less true.

"I don't think that's your intention." Even though she whispered those words, they bounced off the wall like percussion sticks clanging against a cymbal. "But I would be lying if I said I wasn't afraid of that outcome."

She expected to see his face contort into anger at the thought of not getting what he obviously wanted, what she wanted too.

Instead of anger, however, the fire in his eyes softened to a warm glow that seemed to permeate through her skin, soothing the fear that tried to take root inside her.

"Zanai, I want you. I've made no secret of that. But I'm not treating you this way just to get you into bed. I genuinely enjoy spending time in your presence."

Removing his hand from her cheek, he stepped

closer, plucking the champagne glass from her fingers and settling it next to his on the table.

"I won't lie to you and say I'm looking for forever. But whatever this is, one night certainly won't be enough. And even though I'm certain I would enjoy every second of getting to explore your body, it would not define our relationship or convince me to treat you as anything less than the queen I believe you are."

His voice was so husky, his lower register settling over her like a comfy weighted blanket, making her feel safe.

He pulled her to him then, pressing his lips gently against hers as if he were trying to avoid spooking her into retreating. But the way the simple peck made molten fire slide through her veins, singeing every cell in her body, there wasn't a chance in hell she was going to walk away from this.

As if to prove the point to herself, she slid her hands up the front of his chest, loving the way the soft fabric of his Henley clung to his lean but muscular frame, but hating that it kept her from all that glorious flesh beneath it.

Her hands continued their journey until her arms were wrapping around his neck and she was closing any space that dared to stand between them.

He welcomed her into his embrace, sliding his hands from her shoulders down to her waist, pulling her against him in that wonderful way she'd become accustomed to.

She deepened the kiss, needing so desperately to taste him, all of him if he'd let her. The fear of reprisal that seemed to be her constant companion throughout her life seemed to disappear. All that remained was instinct and need, and she surrendered any will she had to deny that fact.

Her tongue licked inside his mouth and he moaned so deep she could feel the rumble of his voice against her chest.

She pulled away slightly, finally breaking the kiss, and lifted her eyes up to him. Her usual need to keep herself hidden was gone. She wanted Jayden to see her. Not just her flesh, but into her heart where hidden emotions she dared not speak, not yet anyway, rested deep in the caverns of her soul.

Panting as she tried to draw life-giving air into her burning lungs, she spoke in a ragged voice. "We're wearing...too many clothes."

He didn't patronize her by asking her if she was sure. The way she was holding onto him for dear life had to convey her desire. But if that didn't, she'd gladly start the process of stripping him where he stood so there was no doubt she wanted him naked and available to her.

"Darlin', that's a problem that's easily fixed." That flirty "devil may care" crooked smile of his was

there and any concerns about this being awkward slipped away.

He pushed her hands down until they were at the bottom of his shirt and she took it from there. She made quick work of pulling it off, and stepped out of her dress even faster.

She was standing there in her lace bra and panties, exposed and nearly naked, but instead of feeling vulnerable, she felt empowered.

His eyes were transfixed, seemingly committing every detail of her form to his memory.

"If you're just going to stare at me all night, this is going to end up being pretty unsatisfying for the both of us."

"See—" he held out a hand to her, pulling her into his strong arms "—that's where you're wrong. I plan to enjoy every damn second of this."

She shivered. That wasn't just a statement, bravado to make himself sound tough and masculine. It was a promise, a vow that they'd both receive unspeakable pleasure from the time they would spend in each other's arms.

As she looked up at him, all she could do was smile. Because for the first time in her life, she was ready to indulge in all the feel-good she could find in his arms.

Jayden struggled to keep his desire in check. They'd made it from the sitting area in their suite to the large king-size bed in his room faster than he could say his name.

Their hands and limbs were everywhere, stripping their remaining clothing. From the first moment he'd laid eyes on her, even behind a mask and a costume, he'd known she'd make him burn for her.

He pulled away from her, needing to slow things down. He'd spent so much time dreaming about this, fantasizing about what it would feel like to finally have her naked under him.

He'd had just a taste of her passion when he'd brought her to climax with his fingers at his condo. But like the old saying went, a taste will only make you mad. Except the madness he'd fought with every fiber of his being had nothing to do with anger, and everything to do with the need he felt all the way down to his cellular level.

He gentled their frenzied kissing, sipping slowly from her lips like he would a fine wine. When she mewled for more, he pulled back, loving the small moan of desperation that crossed her lips.

He kissed the shell of her ear, moving down to the silky skin of her exposed neck that called to him. He grazed it with his teeth, loving the needy shiver that vibrated through her body.

He smoothed eager hands up her sides and around to her slender back, making quick work of the clasp of her bra. When he looked down to find her full flesh practically begging for his attention, his plan to keep things slow so he could savor every inch of her went out the window.

He grasped the back of her thighs, lifting her until her legs were wrapped around his waist as he walked them over to his bed. As soon as she was positioned on the soft bedding, he kissed his way from her full lips charting a path that led down her collarbone, through the valley between her breasts. He was tempted to continue straight down to his prize, but a glimpse of one pert peak drew his attention, detouring his journey.

One flick of his tongue and Zanai arched up seeking more contact. If she wanted more, he would give her more and then some. He alternated between licking, sucking and molding his hands to the shape of her breasts. With the decadent sounds of her pleasure heightening his own, he quickly made his way down her torso, past the natural dip in her waist, until his lips reached her sex.

One gentle pass of his tongue over her clit yielded him a full-body shudder that stoked his own need. Never had a partner's reactions in bed turned him on so much. He didn't dare think about the implications of why that could be so. If he did, he might be tempted to put enough distance between them so he could gain control of himself again, and leaving the cradle of her tempting body wasn't something he could willingly do.

She was so soft, so hot, responsive, her reactions

to his touch were just as heady as the feel of her flesh against his, fueling his need to continue.

He drew slow circles at her entrance with deft fingers as he increased the pressure of his tongue against her clit, slipping one finger in and moaning at the scalding heat that greeted him. His eager cock twitched at the thought of what all that delicious warmth would feel like wrapped around him.

Eager to find out, he added another finger, stroking and scissoring inside her. The sweet sounds of her pleasure filling the room, he focused his efforts, determined she would climax at least once before he satisfied his need to be inside her.

Certain he wouldn't have to wait too long given how her hips were swiveling, matching the rhythm he set with his fingers and his tongue, he added a third finger, stretching her, reveling at the way she possessively wove her digits through his hair, tugging him closer to her. And when her body seized and her ragged voice pierced the silent room, satisfaction spread through him as she broke apart beneath his touch.

He wasted no time pulling away from her. Normally he'd indulge in a moment of just holding her as he watched her come down from her peak. But tonight, he made quick work of finding the condoms he'd packed in anticipation of this moment.

Sheathed, he climbed back onto the bed, taking her mouth in his as he positioned himself at her entrance. It was the only reprieve he could offer considering how her body called to him.

He pushed forward, parting her folds as her heat slowly surrounded him.

"Damn, baby."

The sheer bliss of this moment had him questioning his ability to resist her this long. He'd believed it would be good between them. How could he not when the very sight of her grabbed at something unrecognizable in him?

He tried to sit, be still for a moment, savor the experience of their joining. But she chose that moment to squeeze him, demanding he move and there was no way he could resist.

The next stroke better than the last, he surrendered to their mutual need, driving inside of her until he was buried so deep, he could hardly tell where she began and he ended.

Every stroke, every desperate touch, every tortured sound had Jayden on edge, fighting back a climax that was closing in on him all too soon.

He glanced down at her, finding something akin to mischief flickering in her eyes, and that's when he saw it, the spark of his red queen that he'd met at the masquerade ball.

She wrapped her arms around his neck, pulling him closer to her, locking her legs around his hips, and used his body weight to pivot, switching their positions.

He had been quite all right with being the one in control. He'd assumed it was what Zanai wanted. That apparently was his mistake because the long sigh that escaped her lips as she slid down his length was nearly his undoing.

"Take what you want."

"I plan to."

He couldn't help the smile her declaration garnered.

As she began to move in earnest, driving him closer and closer to the brink, he lost himself in the decadent swivel of her hips and the searing heat of her body encasing his. When his eyes connected with hers, he realized this moment was so much more than just physical pleasure.

There was something that simply delighted his soul to see the indulgent, cocky grin plastered across her face. And when she gazed down at him, giving him a sly wink just before she tightened around him, he was lost. Her release driving him to his own, he raised his hips to meet hers.

Needing more, more contact, more pleasure, more everything, he dreaded the climax closing in on him just as much as he relished it. Too lost to the elusive sensation, he quickly pulled her beneath him. His fierce pace elicited sensual cries so wanton it was like she was somehow reaching inside of him, re-arranging everything he knew to be true about himself and making him into a new creation all her own.

And no matter how scary that thought was, he

couldn't help but hold on to it as she called his name. The sultry sound pushed him over the edge into bliss and he crumbled into a million pieces. He wasn't sure if he could ever be put back together again.

As his body struggled to find its way back to normalcy and the warmth of satisfaction spread through him, he realized he couldn't care less if the scattered pieces of his soul couldn't be reassembled. To be broken by this woman's pleasure was so satisfying, he'd willingly let her violently grind him into dust if it meant he could feel this way again.

He dropped to the bed, pulling her into his side and loving the sense of completion that flooded him as she wrapped herself around him and sighed.

Yeah, he was gone. A fact that should've terrified him. But instead of fear, the only thing he experienced was bone-deep satisfaction.

"When we get back tomorrow, will you be in a rush to get home or can you spare a bit of time?"

She pondered the question from the comfort of the plush bed as he stood at the foot with nothing but a phone in his hand and a towel hanging low around his waist.

"I'm sorry, what did you say? I was a bit distracted by you in a towel."

The naughty gleam in his eye cranked up his sexy factor even more than his exposed carved abs.

"That's good to know that my body distracts you.

I'll have to use that to my advantage sometime soon. But seriously, do you need to rush back home on Sunday when we get back?"

She shook her head. "I'll probably just go over a few case files if nothing else comes up. Why?"

He didn't speak right away, which she could admit, made her slightly concerned so she prodded him again. "Why do you ask?"

He lifted his phone. "My brother just texted me. My parents are having an impromptu cookout and since you'll be there already to pick up your car, you may as well get a plate too."

Whatever she was expecting him to say, it certainly wasn't that.

"Wow, Jayden. You know when Black folks invite you to the cookout, that means you've been accepted into the fold. You sure you want to expose your family to an odd duck like me?"

Her voice had a nervous lilt to it she hoped he'd attribute to her inept attempt at a joke.

"Zanai." The weight of his voice filled the room, pressing hard against her chest, making it increasingly difficult to breathe. "There's nothing odd about you, and I really wish you'd stop saying that. If you hadn't noticed, I'm kind of fond of you, and your self-deprecation aggravates me because I know none of it is true."

"Jayden, I was just joking."

No, she wasn't.

"No, you weren't." She watched him take in a long breath before he spoke again. "I don't know if this is just nerves on your part or Sanford actively working to make you believe that every wealthy person in Royal is a blue-blooded snob who will turn up their nose at you. Either way, it's bullshit and I need you to stop."

His voice was edged with something rough and demanding that should have annoyed her. Instead, it made her feel warm and welcomed.

"There's nothing wrong with you. And there's certainly nothing wrong with you that would give me pause for bringing you around my family. My family is far from perfect. Yet despite our net worth, we've managed to remain a down-home group of folks whose only concern with breeding is for the damn horses on our land. You suggesting otherwise is an insult to them and me."

He closed his eyes for a moment, taking in a slow breath to rein himself in before he continued. "Zanai, you're beautiful, kind, strong and determined. And those are the reasons you can come to the cookout."

By the time she processed what he was saying, she slowly pulled herself up onto her elbows before positioning herself against the pillows adorning the bed. She bore an uncontrollably wide grin on her face that had nothing to do with her excitement over the invitation and everything to do with the man she was talking to.

"Thank you, Jayden." She tried to keep her voice steady so she didn't sound like the grinning idiot her aching face muscles told her that she was. "I'd like very much to come to the cookout."

"Good, we're due to land around noon. That means the ribs should be done and the beer should be cold by the time we get back to the ranch. It's an all-day affair, so if you have anything to wear to work on Monday morning in your bag, you should probably stay at the cottage with me."

"Jayden, it doesn't matter how late it finishes. I can drive myself home. There's no sense in me putting you out."

There was a sinister quality to the wry laugh that billowed from his chest and throat. "I'll have to share you for a good portion of the day with my family. You spending the night means I get to do two of my favorite things: eat my mama's cooking and spend a night pleasing you."

She was about to comment on how sweet and unsettling it was for him to mention sex with her and his mother's cooking in the same breath, but as he placed his phone on the foot bench and crawled up the mattress until he was holding himself above her, the ability to make coherent sentences almost slipped away until her next thought plowed through her lust-dazed brain.

"Are you sure I should stay? I don't need your

mother thinking I'm some trollop trying to corrupt her baby boy."

"Corrupt, huh?"

Goodness, that mischievous grin lifting the edges of his full mouth was like a drug, taking her mind, and hopefully her body, on a trip. "I kinda like the sound of that."

"I just bet you do. But despite your apparent penchant for debauchery, I plan to make a good impression on your family."

"If you insist." They both laughed. At that point she realized it was getting easier and easier to let her guard down around him. She had to admit, it felt good. But part of her wondered just how long she could expect this good thing to last.

He lowered himself on top of her body and she reveled in the heated press of his skin against hers.

She wanted to attribute the strange feeling that seemed to start in the middle of her chest, spreading through her whole system, to the comfort of his weight above her. But deep down, she knew that wasn't it.

Too afraid to name it, she simply delighted in the satisfied sigh that slipped past her lips as his mouth and tongue found the curve of her neck.

"You really are something else, Jayden Lattimore."

He beamed as his hand slid up her thigh, his fingers tightening their grip on the flesh there.

"And don't you forget it."

Eleven

"You're sure your family's okay with you bringing a guest they don't know?"

"Zanai, you're an extra mouth for my mama to feed. She'll never be mad at that. That woman gets joy outta feeding folks I will never understand."

"That's not an answer, Jayden."

He snickered as he pulled up through the opened gates of the Lattimore ranch.

"If you knew my mother, you'd know it really is an answer. My family knows you're coming, Zanai. I've had to threaten each of them to be on their best behavior or suffer my wrath."

She tried to keep a straight face but inside of two

seconds of his declaration, she fell into a bout of laughter. Jayden was the most carefree person she knew. She didn't believe he had the capacity for that kind of anger, to be honest.

"Stop worrying. Everything will be fine. And at some point today, I'm sure someone from the Grandin ranch will probably pop by. We're always infiltrating each other's lands when there's a grill firing up."

That did make her feel better. Although Morgan hadn't mentioned any plans to drop by, Zanai wouldn't be upset if her friend surprised her, providing Zanai with an impromptu wingman to help her ease her way through this gathering.

"You ready?"

She nodded, and put her hand on the door handle, quickly garnering a scowl from him as she did.

"You will not make me look bad in front of my mama by opening your own car door. She taught me better than that."

She tried hard to press her lips into a flat line, but the good mood between them had the corners of her mouth curling despite her efforts to prevent it. "So, you're only being chivalrous because your mother can see?"

He leaned over, stealing a brief kiss before gifting her with a bright smile. "Of course not. I'm way too selfish for that. I'm doing it because it's an excuse to hold your hand when I help you out of the car."

She could feel her amusement tickling the muscles in her face, demanding she smile even when she was trying to maintain a modicum of seriousness.

"You are too slick for your own good."

He stole another kiss. "No such thing." He winked at her, making her heart beat a little faster. He quickly made his way out of the car and to her side, offering her an eager hand to help her out of the vehicle.

He was right, the electric current that zapped through her when his hand connected with hers was more than worth the brief moment she had to wait for him to walk around and open her door.

When she was standing, he took her hand and placed it on his forearm before gifting her with a devilish grin.

"Let's do this."

She nodded, surprised that the unease she usually experienced whenever she was walking into unfamiliar social situations hadn't yet appeared. She could only guess that her mind was so preoccupied with how good it felt to have her hand pressed against him that it didn't have time to freak out about mingling with perfect strangers.

She knew who the Lattimores were, of course. Although there was a lot of wealth in Royal, Texas, there weren't many Black families with the kind of money and prestige the Lattimores possessed.

It would've been impossible not to recognize them. But even though her own father was a wealthy

Black man in this town, there'd been few opportunities for her to mingle with the great Lattimore clan until now.

They walked up the steps and into the large house. The first thing she noticed when she was inside was the warmth that welcomed you once you stepped across the threshold.

From the first time she'd seen the outside of the house when Jayden had invited her over for dinner, she could tell this was a home. There were no marble columns greeting her. Instead, there was a long and wide porch with a swing attached at each end, inviting you to sit down and rest awhile.

She'd known then this was a place where a loving family resided. Walking inside, seeing all the rich burgundy and brown colors, shades that were both bold and soothing, she understood this was a place of comfort and not just a display of how large their bank account was.

They made their way quickly through the large, bright kitchen with its endless counter space stacked with covered aluminum chaffing pans. She couldn't help but be amused at the sight of them. These weren't the expensive kind you saw at the catered events of rich people who wanted to "rough it" by eating outside on the deck or poolside. These were the kind her aunt Déjà up in Brooklyn would get from the local dollar store. She always said the food seemed to cook the best in those pans.

While she was still musing about the novelty of rich folks using cheap pans, they stepped through a slide door that led to an impressive brick-and-stone patio.

It was simple, yet elegant, as was the furniture positioned sparsely throughout the space.

Jayden walked them over to the farthest corner of the patio where his parents were standing. She'd never met Ben and Barbara Lattimore nor any of their remaining three children face-to-face. They were the Lattimores, so of course she knew who each of them was, but this was the first time she'd actually have a proper introduction.

As they approached the grill, Barbara, a sixty-something-year-old woman with a thick and curvy build and dazzling gray hair peppered with a few remaining dark strands, smiled heartily. Even from this considerable distance, Zanai could see the gleam of the woman's bright white teeth.

The simple action put Zanai at ease, stopping the growing ball of nerves that was throbbing in her chest. Meeting the rich and notable could be tricky in these parts. For various reasons, many didn't particularly welcome outsiders. But the exuberance in this woman's eyes made Zanai feel at home before they'd spoken their first words to each other.

Barbara tapped her husband, Ben, on the arm to get his attention. He was a solidly built man, tall, with low-cropped salt-and-pepper hair. She could definitely see how he could be an imposing force if he wanted to be. But when he turned around to see who his wife was pointing to, his dark brown clean-shaven face slipped into the same easy smile his wife wore.

"Mama, Daddy, I'd like you to meet a good friend of mine. This is Dr. Zanai James. Zanai, my parents, Ben and Barbara Lattimore."

Zanai went to extend her hand when Barbara gave it a dismissive shove before opening her arms and tugging Zanai into a warm hug.

When Barbara let her go, Ben wrapped an arm around Zanai's shoulder, tugging her in for a quick side-hug.

"Hello, Mr. and Mrs. Lattimore. Thank you for welcoming me into your lovely home."

"Look here, young lady." Ben's terse tone was belied by the broad grin on his face. "We don't stand on ceremony 'round here. I'm Ben and this is Barbara."

"He's right," Barbara continued. "You're among friends. So go grab you a plate and pile up on some of that food over there on the table. As soon as we're done with these ribs, we'll come join you."

Zanai reciprocated their friendly smiles. "Thank you. I look forward to it."

"Are Grandma and Grandpa around? I want to introduce them."

His father shook his head and a flash of sadness sparked in his eyes. "Your grandpa was a bit flustered, so Grandma took him upstairs for a nap. If he's feeling better, I'm sure they'll be down later."

Jayden nodded, then walked her over to the long, rectangular table where more covered aluminum pans rested.

They made quick work of filling their plates, giving her only a short moment to glance up and see the calm happiness that seemed to settle over Jayden.

Even from his profile she could see he was more relaxed. He was a laid-back person by nature, but here, he seemed even more comfortable if that were possible. With heavy plates and bottles of water in hand, they turned toward a long picnic bench in the middle of the deck where Jayden's older brother, younger sisters and three people she knew were his siblings' love interests from her conversations with Morgan sat watching them walk over.

"Zanai, this is my brother, Jonathan, and his better half, Natalie. This is my sister Alexa and her shadow, Jackson, and this is Caitlyn and her beau, Dev. Y'all, this is Dr. Zanai James."

"Doctor, huh?" That came from Alexa, a slender brown-skinned beauty with a long mane of jet-black curls. If it wasn't for the teasing gleam in her eye, her question might've put Zanai on edge. "That means you're smart, right?" Not waiting for Zanai to answer she continued, "So please explain what the hell you're doing with this guy."

Zanai couldn't help the honest snicker that bubbled up her throat and leapt out of her mouth. "Well, he makes me laugh. That in and of itself is a priceless skill."

Jonathan's eyes widened as he extended his hand to Zanai. "You hear that, Jay? She actually thinks you're worth something. That's a first."

He playfully winked at Zanai before shaking her hand. "I'm his older, much more handsome brother, Jonathan. It's very nice to finally meet you up close and personal."

"Ditto what he said," Alexa interjected. "We've seen you around town with Morgan, but I don't think any of us have ever had the chance to actually interact with you."

Royal was a small town, even Zanai couldn't manage to go completely unnoticed in it. "I'm a bit of a homebody. Being out and about in Royal can be a bit much for me."

"I can certainly understand that." Caitlyn gave her a delicate hand to shake. "Being around people takes up a lot of energy I don't always have."

Caitlyn patted an empty spot on the bench next to her. Getting the feeling Zanai had just stumbled on to a kindred spirit, she accepted the invitation and sat down next to Caitlyn while Jayden sat on the opposite side of the table where Alexa and Jonathan sat.

"Don't you pity me now that you see what I have to contend with when I'm around these folks?"

Pity him? No, pity wasn't what she'd call this feeling at all. Even as she smiled and enjoyed the good-natured ribbing that only became more robust once his parents joined the table, Zanai didn't pity Jayden. She envied him.

As his family made jokes at his expense, there was this unmistakable thread of love that connected them all.

Zanai had never been part of something like that, not even when her mother was alive. Witnessing the simple way a family interacted when they loved each other scratched at the secret longing she'd carried for years. But even as she ached for this kind of affection in her own family, watching it play out so easily amongst the Lattimores made warmth radiate throughout her body.

I could get used to this.

The thought was like pouring ice-cold water down her spine. No matter how nice this was, she couldn't allow herself to get accustomed to it. Jayden was here for the fun and nothing more. To forget that would be the worst mistake she could make.

As if he could sense there was an unspoken shift in her, he tossed a slightly concerned look across the table, silently asking if she were all right.

She wasn't. Not when everything she'd ever dreamed of having was sitting right here at this table. Life had already taught her this sort of happiness wasn't for her. But the draw of Jayden's smile and the shared laughter of his family dragged her back into this pool of good feelings and comfort. It was so powerful, her brain kept screaming at her to get out while she still had the chance, while she still could protect herself.

She took a deep breath, putting on her best smile and nodding, hoping he couldn't detect her reservation any longer. No matter how dangerous this was, she couldn't pretend she wasn't enjoying every second of it.

So, as warning bells in her head went off, she willfully ignored them, grabbing her fork and tucking into the potato salad on her plate—which she was certain was the best she'd ever tasted. She'd pay for that act later, of that, she was sure. But for right now, consequences be damned, she allowed this close-knit family to submerge her in their sincerity.

The sky was turning dusk. Usually, he loved a good sunset as much as the next person who treasured the wide-open spaces in Royal. But tonight, each inch the sun dropped below the horizon meant he was closer to tomorrow arriving and Zanai leaving for work. He just didn't want that.

"What's on your mind, little brother?" Jonathan's voice intruded on his thoughts, making him pull his attention away from Zanai as she sat with his sisters talking.

"Nothing."

"You may have that pretty therapist smitten, but not me. What are you really thinking?"

As much shit as Jonathan gave him, he was a great big brother to Jayden. He'd always been there, always had his back. If there were anyone in this world who he could share his thoughts with, it was him. Not to mention, Jonathan's ability to find something good with Natalie after going through hell during his marriage to his ex also made him the ideal person to have this conversation with.

"Honestly, I don't know."

"This woman has you that twisted up, huh?"

"We're really just having fun, Jonathan. But I'd be lying if I said I wanted it to end anytime soon. There's just something about her that makes me want to keep her close."

His brother hung a playful arm around Jayden's neck and pulled him into a half hug, half headlock. "Then go with it. Do like you usually do and enjoy it. Don't overthink it."

His brother was right. Jayden was king of letting things unfold as they naturally would. But in this case, for some reason his head hadn't clued in yet. The idea of not doing something to ensure this feeling lasted didn't sit right with him.

He was so uncomfortable with the idea, he was itchy and tight in his own skin thinking about it. Deep down he knew that just letting things happen as they were supposed to could mean this good thing he was enjoying more than he should would eventually disappear from his life.

He leaned into his brother's hug, turning and pulling Jonathan into his embrace. "Thanks, man."

"Anytime."

He disengaged from his brother's arms and walked over to Zanai. He tilted his head toward the other end of the patio, and she quickly followed his lead, excusing herself from his sisters.

"You ready to go?"

She gave him a weary smile. "No, actually. I'm having a great time. But it is getting late, and I should probably get some rest before I turn into a pumpkin."

"I'm sure you'd make the prettiest pumpkin in all of Royal."

"You're either drunk or on your way to a sugar coma after all that sweet potato pie you were putting away."

"Nope, we've been here for about four hours and I've only had two beers and I've eaten more than a football team, so I'm completely sober."

He slid his hand down her arm until he was linking his fingers with hers. They remained that way as they said their goodbyes and made their way to the front of the house where his car was parked.

"Did you really enjoy yourself?"

There was a tenderness that settled over her face as the apples of her cheeks rose with her smile.

"I did. Your family is amazing, by the way. Thank

you for inviting me. I didn't realize how much I needed a day like this."

"You're busy helping people who need it. You deserve a day of fun and food."

They finally reached his car, but instead of reaching for the door so she could pull her overnight bag from the back seat, she brought her soft brown gaze up to his. Even in the dim lights that illuminated the driveway during the night, he could see something burning in her eyes that made his skin tingle and his cock twitch.

"You really need to stop looking at me like that."

"Like what?"

He couldn't tell if the innocent expression on her face was real or a ruse. Either way, it made desire lick at his insides, making him desperate to touch her no matter if they had privacy or not.

"Like you want something I desperately want to give you."

Initially, he thought his response must have shocked her. That was the only way he could make sense of the slight drop in her jaw resulting in her mouth opening just the smallest bit. But then his eyes traveled down the length of her face to her graceful neck and he saw her pulse jumping just beneath her skin.

Zanai was a slim woman, but even with her build, if her pulse was visible, her heart had to be drumming along at a fierce rhythm.

Drawn to it, he lifted his hand, allowing his thumb to caress the area. No, he wasn't touching her in a clinical manner like a medical professional would. He was gently dragging his thumb back and forth across the spot, searching for much more than signs of life, but signs of the same need burning through his own cells.

Without thinking, he snaked his fingers around the back of her neck, pulling her to him as he pressed his lips to hers. They were outside, in the view of any of his family who might've chosen that moment to walk by. But the fire growing inside him once his flesh met hers was too great to be concerned with things like getting caught by nosy onlookers.

That was especially true once she inched her fingers up the sizzling skin of his arms, her palms lying flat against his shoulders before snaking around his neck, keeping him pressed against her.

It was a bold move for someone as reserved as Zanai and the thought that she was so turned on she'd forget herself in an open space did unspeakable things to him. It made his already-scorching blood boil, the resulting pressure racing through his body looking for an outlet, finding none save for his cock, making it twitch with more than simple interest, but need.

The sparks they ignited turned into a burning flame. If he had common sense, he'd retreat to safety, putting as much distance between him and her as possible. However, his brain was too filled with the haze of lust to allow for any pragmatism. Instead, he gripped her hips, loving the natural curves that seemed to fit perfectly in his hands, tugging her to him so she could feel exactly what she was doing to him.

A long moan trickled across her lips and into the night air, charging it with need. He kissed her harder, walking her backward until she was against his car. He pulled his lips from hers, placing a path of kisses from her chin to the shell of her ear.

"You have no idea how much I want you."

His voice was raspy, as if he'd been drinking or yelling for so long that the delicate flesh of his throat was rubbed raw from overuse.

"Actually, I'm pretty sure I do." She flexed her hips, pressing against his stiffening cock. Surprised by her forwardness, he worried if this was too much for her and he should pull away. But then she slipped one hand around the base of his neck while placing the other at his waist, tugging him against her.

When his eyes dropped down to hers, he saw a fire matching the one he knew burned within him and any doubts he had of pushing her too far too fast melted away.

This wasn't the reserved woman who protected herself by separating herself from the world. This was the fierce woman he'd had the pleasure of dancing with at the masquerade ball.

He'd seen glimpses of her in the time he and Zanai had spent together. But tonight was the first time he'd seen her willingly come out to play without being coaxed.

"Darlin', we'd better make a move because whether we're here in the driveway or back in my cottage, I'm going to experience what it is to have my naked flesh covered with yours again."

She moaned, wrapping both arms around his neck and draping herself over him. "Trust me, Jayden. It can't be soon enough for me."

He nuzzled her neck, gently nibbling the exposed flesh there and smiling at the needy tremor that racked her body as he did so.

"I would love for it to be this very second," he said as he pressed her against his car, loving how her body molded to his. "I can only imagine how beautiful you'd look spread across the hood of this car. But since my mama is only a stone's throw away from us, that ain't happening tonight."

"You're such a tease for putting that image in my head and not following through."

"Dr. James, I do believe I've corrupted you."

"I'm pretty sure you have."

He bent down to kiss her again, needing to taste her sweetness one more time.

"Good to know, but since I'm not exactly prepared, we're still gonna have to take this show inside."

She pulled back from him and he could see eagerness that made his heart race like a shot of adrenaline.

"If you mean condoms, I have those."

He placed a sweet kiss on her lips, chuckling as he answered her. "Look at you being all prepared." She offered him a smile in return, soothing some of the burn he believed would eventually consume him if they didn't stop now.

"I'm very glad to know you're prepared for the fun we'll get into. However, I wasn't talking about condoms. I keep telling you, you're a queen. You're not someone to be used in a disposable way. Every time I'm buried inside you again, I plan to show you it means something to me. So, as much as my flesh is willing, I'm going to calm my ass down, drive you to my cottage and worship you the way you deserve."

He could see the disappointment sliding down her face like an ominous cloud. Part of him was delighted for it. No, he didn't want to see her needs and wants go unmet even for a brief moment. But, if she was this visibly disappointed and impatient, that meant she was just as into the idea of them recreating the magic they experienced in New York.

"Don't worry, my queen. This is a good thing."

She shrugged, tilting her head as she looked up at him, trying to analyze his meaning.

"I don't see how getting me this aroused and then not doing anything about it is a good thing."

His hands tightened on the curve of her hips, and

he released a desperate groan into the air. Hearing her speak of her arousal was just another thing to make him burn for her.

"I plan to do everything about it. Just not right this minute. Besides, you do realize that all the time we've spent yammering at my car, we could've been back to the cottage already playing at my new favorite activity."

She looked up, giving him a sultry smile that raised his ardor one more tick above scorching.

"Oh, yeah, and what exactly is your new favorite activity?"

"Pleasing you." The words slipped through his mouth without any hesitation, a fact that if he were honest, unnerved him a bit. This wasn't part of his usual MO. He was a "love 'em and leave 'em, content when he walked away" kind of guy. He kept things light. But as he stood there watching her, his body beside itself with need, even he couldn't delude himself long enough to ignore the fact that this was in no way keeping it light.

The worst part of it all was, there, somewhere deep inside of him, he was actually glad about that. And therein lay the problem. How deep had he fallen if he actually wanted to keep her near?

She pulled him to her, pressing soft lips against him, licking inside his mouth in a bold maneuver that made him fight to keep his control, and in that moment, he realized he didn't care how far he'd fallen.

The only thing he cared about was keeping her with him for as long as he could.

Too lost in her touch to contemplate the future disaster he knew this could pose, he decided he wouldn't borrow tomorrow's trouble. Tonight, he'd allow himself to become intoxicated by the woman in his arms. A fact he was certain he would surely pay for later.

Twelve

They'd barely made it inside his cottage before they were tearing each other's clothes off. They took a brief reprieve to retrieve a condom from Zanai's bag, and as soon as the foil pack was in her grasp, they were plastered against each other again.

Too eager to be inside of her, he moved them toward the large sofa in the middle of his living room. They hastily discarded their last few articles of clothing. Jayden stopped for a moment. Standing behind her, he kissed the elegant curve at the base of her neck as his hands gripped her hips.

She was delicate, yet so strong. It hardly made sense to him that this woman had so much power over him. Whether she knew it or not, she was fast becoming an addiction for Jayden. He had his reservations, but the truth was, he was more and more willing to step off this emotional cliff she had him on if it meant bringing them both the pleasure they craved.

Refusing to let his thoughts temper the heat blazing between them, he encouraged her to climb onto the cushions until she was leaning forward with her front against its back.

"What is it with you and couches?"

He moaned softly, leaning down to nip at her earlobe with his teeth before whispering, "If you could see the view I have from back here, you'd get why there's no place I'd rather be than here with you spread across this very sturdy piece of furniture."

Before she could respond, he sheathed himself, plastering himself against her back before sliding his eager fingers over her hip, then between her folds. Her slick heat seared the pads of his fingers and he had to brace himself to keep from toppling onto her.

"Is all this for me?" He delighted in the shudder that passed through as he pressed two fingers inside her.

When she moaned as he slid his fingers in and out, he nearly came right there.

"No, it's for me. Now get on with it."

"So bossy."

"And you love it."

"Damn straight, I do."

He did as the lovely woman commanded, positioning himself at her entrance, slowly entering her from behind to give her body a chance to adjust to him.

When she dropped her head against the back of the couch, and pushed back against him, that was all the encouragement he needed.

With one knee bent on the sofa cushions and the other foot planted firmly on the ground, he gripped her shoulder with one hand and her hip with the other before he sank home.

That word wasn't just a euphemism either. Not the way her sex cradled him, gripping him so tightly, and certainly not the way she moaned with unadulterated want as he moved inside of her.

After a few slow strokes, he finally gave her what they both wanted, increasing his pace. She was close already. Her tight heat quivered around him, and he could tell she was trying her best to hold out, to deny the climax that was sneaking up on them both.

"Let go," he whispered as he covered her back with his chest. "Give in."

He dropped his hand from her hip, circling firm fingers around her clit until she cried out, falling headlong into her release.

Her body was tight and her jaw slack as she called out his name. She buried her face into the cushions, muffling the sounds as she continued to fall apart beneath his touch.

The sounds she was making poured gasoline on the inferno already threatening to consume them. There was no way he could resist taking his own pleasure soon.

He pulled her upright, planting a demanding kiss on her full lips before burying himself into her again.

He released her long enough to position her with her head on the armrest and her ass in the air, put on display just for him. The sight she made, like she was a gift waiting just for him, it tugged at every lecherous part of his personality, calling him to bury himself in her and finish this torture once and for all.

He positioned himself behind her, slamming into her, loving the loud litany of the word *yes* on repeat as his flesh slapped against hers, making the obscene sound of slick need their bodies created.

He could feel her spasming again, bearing down on his flesh in the most delicious way, triggering his peak. The electric shock waking up every nerve he possessed until his entire being felt alive. He rode that high until Zanai's demanding body clenched around him, and then he was lost.

Jayden's stride faltered as the tension of his climax built until it was a dramatic wave looming above him, its power both inviting and daunting. And at the very last possible moment when his mind shut down and his body took over, he surrendered himself to the inevitable force of his orgasm taking hold of him while the unrelenting pleasure her body offered consumed him.

He collapsed under its weight, falling against her back, circling his arms tightly around her chest as the waves of his climax pulsed through him.

When it was over, and he could finally find the clarity and the strength to swim back to cognizance, his muscles gave way. With exhaustion pulling him down against her back and into oblivion, he used the last bit of his strength to separate from her body, dispose of the condom and pull her on top of his chest. Circling his arms possessively around her, he swiped a lock of hair out of her face, cupping her chin as he stared into her satisfied gaze.

"We are definitely doing that again." His utterance garnered a sleepy smile from her just before she dropped her head to his chest and snuggled against him.

"We damn sure are."

"Details, please."

Zanai blinked, slightly dazed by the whirlwind that was her best friend, Morgan. The last time she'd seen Morgan had been before she and Jayden had left for New York and before he'd brought her home to meet his family. That seemed so long ago.

The beautiful redhead appeared so abruptly, that Zanai had to look around the local coffee shop to see if any other guests were swept up in her friend's tailwinds.

"Spill what? The coffee I was just about to take a sip of?"

Morgan crossed her arms, her lips poking out without the slightest hint of amusement anywhere on her face.

"Zanai, I'm tired and irritable. While I was dealing with a busy store and annoying customers, you were off jet-setting with the very handsome Jayden Lattimore. I need details, and I need them now."

Zanai's laughter bubbled up, escaping her lips, and she was rewarded with a sharply raised brow from her best friend.

"I'd hardly call going to New York for the weekend 'jet-setting.'"

Morgan huffed, "Fine, does gallivanting work better for you?"

"You really are in a mood today. Everything okay?"

Morgan took a breath, some of her irritability bleeding out with the long sigh she expelled.

"I'll be fine. Like I said, the store was really busy this weekend and I'm just feeling a little tired. I won't dare complain, though. It's better to be run ragged with paying customers than to sit in an empty store."

Zanai saw a glimmer of her friend's usual upbeat personality shining through, helping her relax a bit.

"Enough about me, though. I don't have a lot of

time before I'll need to get back. I just wanted to catch up with you and see how your weekend went."

"It was fine."

That amusement that seemed nonexistent a few moments ago seemed to crack through Morgan's stiff countenance, resulting in a wicked grin on Morgan's face.

"Fine, my foot. What happened?"

Zanai sipped from her cup of coffee slowly just to get on Morgan's nerves. When she saw Morgan's brow knit, that was Zanai's cue that she'd taken things a bit too far.

"All right already. It was wonderful. We saw a play, had lunch in a really fancy restaurant and spent most of the night drinking champagne and getting naked in his hotel room."

Morgan's face lit up, her excitement over Zanai's account of her weekend activities chasing away the clouds of annoyance shadowing her bright eyes.

"Way to go, Jayden. I'm glad he's pulling out all the stops for you."

"All the stops? We spent a night in New York. I'd hardly call that anything spectacular."

Morgan didn't respond. Well, not verbally anyway. Her shaking head and tightly set mouth did all the talking for her.

"We both know Royal is a small town. If he were whisking any other resident away from here for overnight trips to New York, there's no way we wouldn't have heard about it by now. The only reason it isn't all over town already is that you're not a gossip and I would never betray your confidence like that."

A fact Zanai was most grateful for. The last thing she needed was this town, and by extension her father and his wife, finding out about her and Jayden. If things kept up the way they were, she knew it would eventually get back to Sanford. But for now, while it was still in its new and shiny stage, she wanted to savor this before the complication of her father became part of the equation.

"I think it's obvious Jayden really likes you."

Goodness, Zanai hoped so. The attention he paid her, the time they spent together, she'd been desperately afraid she was just seeing what she wanted to see. Although she knew it wouldn't be a lasting thing, to know that he genuinely wanted to be around her made her heart stumble in her chest.

"I like him too."

"And that scares you why?"

Zanai could feel the smile dripping from her face as Morgan spoke. When two people were as close as them, trying to hide anything was a fruitless exercise.

"Jayden is great and I enjoy his company immensely."

"But?"

"Eventually this will end and he'll find another woman to charm."

Her friend placed a comforting hand on top of hers, soothing the ache that Zanai wanted desperately to ignore.

"And you're okay with that?"

"I'll have to be. No sense in getting all worked up over something that isn't real. Instead, I'm just going to enjoy this wonderful man for as long as I can. I deserve that much."

For the first time in her life, Zanai actually believed those words. She deserved to be treated well. She knew it as intrinsically as she knew her own name.

"You deserve more than that."

Zanai nodded. "I know."

Morgan's face lit up with a soft smile that warmed Zanai's entire being much more than the few sips of coffee she'd had.

"For the first time ever, I honestly believe you know that's true."

"Using the photograph you supplied, I was able to come up with a comparable likeness for the piece you commissioned."

Jayden smiled as he sat in a private room at the jeweler's. Mr. Danbury had offered to come out to the ranch to complete their business, but if his family saw the town jeweler on the premises, they'd jump to all sorts of conclusions he wasn't ready to acknowledge yet.

Mr. Danbury uncovered a velvet tray with a delicate platinum necklace with ruby and diamond teardrops. It was the perfect match to the earrings and bracelet Zanai had worn the night of the masquerade ball.

He couldn't say exactly why he'd felt the need to have this piece commissioned. They hadn't really been dating that long or seriously enough that expensive pieces of jewelry were warranted. But for some reason beyond even his own understanding, he wanted something of his close to her person. Something that would touch her, physically and emotionally, reminding her of how special he thought she was.

"Is it to your liking, Mr. Lattimore?"

Jayden blinked slightly, almost forgetting he wasn't alone in the dimly lit room.

"Mr. Danbury, it's perfect. Would you put it in a pretty box for me?"

"Most certainly, Mr. Lattimore."

Jayden paid for his purchase and waited patiently as Mr. Danbury placed the velvet jewelry box into a red gift box. When the gentleman placed it in Jayden's hand, he smiled as unexpected happiness began to bloom.

He didn't question it. He didn't even chastise himself for going too far too fast where Zanai was concerned. He just rode the high of good feelings rushing through his system as he left the shop, heading for his car parked a few doors down.

"Did you get anything pretty for my daughter while you were in with Danbury?"

Jayden's eyes focused on the tall man with brown skin dressed in a charcoal business suit and a black Stetson. He was leaning on Jayden's car, looking every bit the part of a Black J.R. Ewing with a deceptively sweet smile and easy manner.

"I'm sorry, Mr. James, I'm not sure I understand your meaning."

Sanford kept his pleasant smile pasted to his face as he stood to his full height, nearly reaching Jayden's eye level.

"The piece of jewelry you just bought from Danbury. I assume it's for my daughter Zanai, right?"

The hairs on the back of Jayden's neck stood up, prickling his neckline as he focused on Sanford's words.

"With all due respect, Mr. James, I'm not certain how what I do or don't buy and for whom I buy it is a matter that concerns you."

Jayden watched as the slick smile on Sanford's face began to slip as the man stepped closer to him.

"If it has to do with my daughter, it definitely concerns me. Especially since you've been occupying so much of her time and taking her to New York for special getaways."

Jayden's gaze narrowed as he glared at Sanford. "Are you having us followed?"

The older man scoffed, but didn't answer. Pushing Jayden further to the edge of his building anger.

Jayden didn't flinch, he held remarkably still as Sanford scanned him for a reaction. If he was waiting for Jayden to be ashamed, he'd wait for a mighty long time. Jayden had proudly enjoyed every moment he'd spent with Zanai, including those carefree times in New York.

"What do you want, Sanford?"

Jayden had had just about enough of whatever this nonsense was. He'd lost all his home training about two seconds ago. To make sure this stayed civil, he needed to end this sooner rather than later.

"I like a man that's direct. Your daddy taught you well, boy."

Sanford's cold laugh made the warm Texas air around him drop as if Jayden had walked into a meat locker.

"I want to know what your game is, young man. We both know my daughter isn't your type. She's awkward, and she's not cultured, and she wouldn't know how to land, let alone keep, a man like you if her life depended on it. So I have to wonder then why you'd waste time and money wooing her when she's so far out of her league. Are you planning to use her to get to me?"

At that, Jayden's neck snapped back as if Sanford

had physically struck him. He may as well have considering how shocking the blow of his words was.

"What on earth could I possibly gain from using Zanai to get to you? I've barely said two words to you for the decade and a half you've been in this town. Why would you suddenly be the target of such a dubious plan?"

Sanford shoved his hands in his pockets, still keeping his gaze locked with Jayden's, not giving an inch in his accusatory stance.

"We both know I'm a hell of a lot richer than I was when I came to this town. Maybe you and that family of yours have decided there were too many of us skin-folks walking around in the same tax bracket. Perhaps the job fell to you to set a honeypot trap for my daughter to infiltrate me and my business. If that's the case, it won't work. I wouldn't let that mealymouthed, incompetent child of mine near any of my business matters. So your efforts are wasted."

Jayden held his jaw so tightly, grinding his teeth together so hard that it ached as if he'd been belted by something much harder than any man's right hook.

Jayden was the most easygoing of all his parents' children. But that also meant when he was pissed, he was much more likely to lose his temper and do something stupid like slapping the taste out of this man's mouth.

He could feel every muscle in his body tense and his hands ball tightly into fists at his side. He stepped closer to Sanford, watching the older man shiver just slightly as he did.

That's real good, Sanford. You do have self-preservation instincts after all.

"For the life of me I couldn't understand why such a beautiful, accomplished and compassionate woman couldn't seem to understand her own power. But two seconds of you in my face, and it's so clear. The problem isn't her. It's you."

Something dark flashed across Sanford's face. He looked like a cornered animal filled with a mixture of fear and anger. This was probably a good time for Jayden to walk away, but he couldn't. And there was only one reason that made him stand in this slimy excuse for a human being's presence any longer than it took to wipe crap off the bottom of his shoe.

Zanai.

"Whatever Zanai and I share is none of your business. She's a grown woman and is more than capable of making her own decisions."

Sanford swallowed and stepped back. The simple move gave Jayden sincere satisfaction. It was the moment a bully recognized he'd met his match.

"You don't want to make an enemy out of me, boy." The diminution didn't have the same bite as it had previously. Not with the almost imperceptible quiver in Sanford's voice.

"I think you'll find we're more evenly matched

than you believed, Sanford. Take me on at your own risk."

When he couldn't scare Jayden, Sanford slipped his faux smile on his face again. "I'm trying to do you a favor, son. A man like you can't afford to get tied up with the wrong woman. You wouldn't want all that family prestige to go down the drain because my daughter can't hack it in your circles. She's—"

Jayden stepped close enough to Sanford that he could smell the scent of stale cigarettes on his breath.

"One more word, Sanford. That's what you've got. One more negative comment about Zanai and I'm going to lose the manners my mama taught me."

What little bit of self-preservation Sanford had must have kicked in, because he stepped back, making sure he was more than an arm's length away from Jayden.

Smart man.

"Who don't hear will feel, Jayden. Who don't hear will feel. Remember I tried to warn you."

Jayden stood stock-still for a few minutes after Sanford disappeared from his view. He needed that time to get his head together. He needed to talk to Zanai, tell her about what was going on. But before he could do that, he had to get his anger in check.

Sanford might be an asshole, but he was still her father, and if he didn't handle this well, it could become a wedge between them. They were finally getting closer, and the thought of losing Zanai over this made his anger bleed into fear. He couldn't lose her, not when he was so close to having everything he wanted.

Once he'd calmed down enough that his heartbeat wasn't thumping in his ears, he realized his phone was vibrating in his back pocket.

Without looking at the screen or putting on any of the usual charm he used when greeting folks, he answered the call with a short "yeah."

"Okay, who spit in your Cap'n Crunch today?"

The sound of Alexa's voice mentioning his favorite childhood cereal cracked through the residual anger lingering after Sanford's departure.

He huffed softly, trying to find his center again. "You know I don't play when it comes to the Cap'n."

"Trust me, we all know how ballistic you would go if one of us dared to eat your diabetes in a box."

He playfully grumbled. "I know you didn't call me to talk about my superior choices in breakfast cereals. What's up?"

"You sure you okay? You sounded a little off when you answered the phone."

He didn't want to rehash his conversation with Sanford. It would only serve to piss him off again.

"I'm fine. What do you need?"

Alexa's breathing became audible through the line.

"You need to get back to the ranch as soon as possible. Jonas Shaw called. He's coming over to update us on his investigation into Heath Thurston's claim."

A new irritation settled in his bones. But this went deeper than the blind rage he felt boiling up when Sanford was warning him off of Zanai. That made him angry. This, however, worried him.

Whatever Jonas Shaw had to say, it could very well mean the loss of part of his family's ranch. Jayden didn't want to entertain that idea. But like everything else concerning this entire convoluted issue, it didn't look as if life was going to give him much of a choice.

Thirteen

Jayden walked into the family room finding his three siblings, their parents and their neighbors, the Grandins, sitting with Jonas Shaw, the private investigator they'd hired to dig into this problem.

"All right, what did you find out?"

"Jayden, there's no need to be rude. Where are your manners?" His mother's voice held that sharp tone it had when she was chastising him as a kid.

"I'm sorry." He cleared his throat before taking the empty seat next to Alexa on one of the large sofas in the family room. "Hello, everybody." When everyone in the room acknowledged his greeting, he turned to the investigator. "Jonas. Do you have any news for us?"

Jonas gave him a reassuring smile, as if he understood Jayden's lapse in manners.

"Yes, Jayden. I do have news. But I'm not sure it will do anything but raise more questions."

His father sat stoic in his favorite armchair. The stern look reminding him of how serious he'd looked when all this nonsense with Thurston's claim had begun.

"I talked to the old surveyor," Jonas began, hedging his cadence as if to soften the blow of whatever he was about to tell them. "Henry Lawrence checked his paperwork and confirms there's no oil on the land." He picked up a folder and handed it to Jayden's father, Ben.

"This is a copy of Lawrence's records. It's all right there. There's nothing on either side of the land that would've warranted Victor Senior and Augustus turning over rights. The rights are useless."

"You said there's no oil on the land now. Was there ever any?" Jonathan asked.

Jayden could tell everyone else in the room was thinking along the same lines as Jonathan was.

"No," Jonas answered.

"I honestly can't make any sense of this," Jayden said.

Alexa nodded as she responded, "That's because it doesn't make any sense. If there's no oil, why would Augustus and Victor Senior sign over the rights?"

Jonas shrugged. "I'm afraid the only person who

can give you any real answers is your grandfather, Augustus. If he can't tell you anything, then…"

"…then my grandfather, Victor Senior, took those secrets to the grave," Vic continued.

"Is everything okay?"

Zanai rushed across the threshold of Jayden's cottage as soon as he opened the door. He'd called her as usual just as she was leaving work. Expecting one of their playful chats, Jayden's stern voice filtered through her car's speakers instead, falling heavy against her chest as he asked her to come see him immediately.

"Jayden, is everything all right? Is anyone hurt?"

His penetrating gaze cut through her, pinning her to the spot in his foyer she was currently occupying as she waited for him to respond.

"No one's hurt." The belt of fear his voice had tightened around her heart loosened the slightest bit. But the stiff set of his jaw, the way his bright brown eyes had deepened into a muddy brown, still concerned her. This wasn't Jayden, at least not the Jayden she'd come to know and care for.

"It's been a rough day. Remember how I told you about Heath Thurston's oil claim against the adjoining land between us and the Grandins?"

She nodded. He'd given her a brief rundown of it when he'd invited her to the cookout. Although serious, it didn't seem to weigh on him as heavily as it did now.

"Has something changed?"

"Regrettably, no." His eyes softened a bit as he huffed, exasperation rolling off him in waves.

"My family's trying to sort out some issues with our land. We thought we'd have a lead today from our private investigator, but the so-called lead just brought more questions."

"I'm sorry, Jayden. This must be so frustrating to all of you."

She raised a gentle hand to his face, letting her thumb slide across the tight line of his stubble-covered jaw.

He covered her hand with his own, leaning into her touch as if it was a much-needed balm for all that was ailing him.

He took her hand in his and pressed a light kiss to her palm before leading her out of the foyer and bringing them to the large leather sofa in the center of the living room.

"Make no mistake," he continued, "this is a pain in the ass that could have some serious consequences if we can't get to the bottom of what's going on. As much as it concerns me, that's not why I asked you to come here."

Zanai tilted her head, letting her eyes slide up and down his form, then back again as she tried to deci-pher his meaning.

"Zanai, did you tell Sanford about us?"

Her eyelids seemed to be stuck on rapid blink mode as she tried to process his question.

"No. Why would I?"

Now it was her turn to be stiff as she braced for whatever Jayden would say next.

"To be clear, it wouldn't matter to me if you had. I'm not ashamed of anything we've done and you shouldn't be either. We're not a dirty little secret you need to keep."

She shook her head, pulling back, attempting to get a better understanding of whatever he was trying to tell her.

"Once you brought me to meet your family, I didn't think you were all that concerned about who knew about us. I've never felt like we were secret." She wrapped her fingers in his, needing the connection to help her feel anchored. Fear had robbed her of so much in her life, she didn't want Jayden to be one more thing it tarnished for her.

"Jayden, what's going on?"

"Sanford cornered me when I was in town today. He wanted me to know that he was aware we were seeing each other and he warned me to stay away from you."

Ice spread through her veins at the mention of her father's name. No good had or would ever come from her father showing interest in anything in her life.

She fought the cold panic trying to take over. If

she froze up, she'd never be able to think her way out of whatever Sanford was planning.

Think, Zanai. Think.

"How did he know? We've been around town having meals, but we haven't been overly affectionate in Royal. How could he possibly know?"

"He somehow knew we were in New York. I asked if he was following us. He wouldn't answer."

She fought to crush the full-body tremor threatening to rip through her being. Something dark and angry settled in his eyes and for the briefest moment, she couldn't tell if it was a residual effect from meeting with her father, or if that glare was directed at her.

"We both know that Sanford isn't the loving, protective type when it comes to me. So if you're angry enough that you're damn near grinding your teeth together, he had to have said or done something more than announce his knowledge of our relationship. What happened, Jayden?"

He moved closer. His body was still stiff with the barely concealed anger thrumming through it. But even though he was obviously out of sorts, his nearness calmed some of the anxiety her brain was having a hard time curbing.

"He told me to stay away from you. I would've understood it if he were just a father being protective of his daughter. But there was something sinister about it. He accused me of sleeping with you to somehow sabotage his business and get insider information. He didn't seem to care that I'm a rancher and the only businesses that concern me are those connected to land and livestock."

She dropped her head, shame pressing down on her back and shoulders so heavily, all she could do was slump down into the sofa cushions.

"I'm so sorry, Jayden. He was so out of line. He had no right to say something like that to you. I hope you know I don't believe you could ever be so callous. You would never do that to me."

He leaned over and kissed her gently, as if he understood if he offered her anything more, the dam would break.

"I know you trust me, Zanai. And I would never violate that trust by using you like that." He squeezed her hand to reassure her his words were true. "I'm not the least bit concerned about Sanford's baseless accusations."

He dropped his gaze before he spoke again. "Listen, Zanai," he started, then closed his eyes before continuing, as if whatever he had to say was so heavy, so difficult that he couldn't even look at her as the words dropped from his lips.

Worry crawled up her spine as she attempted to anticipate what he wanted to say.

"I know he's your father, but no one should have to put up with his crap."

The fear tightening around the bottom of her spine

increased the pressure of its grip, numbing her from everything except the despair that was now spreading throughout the rest of her body.

He's leaving me.

The thought was so clear in her head, she worried she had spoken the words out loud. But since Jayden didn't react, she figured she'd kept them locked away.

Her chest hurt, like a vise was crushing her, preventing her from taking a breath. She'd known he'd eventually leave. She'd known from the very beginning she was a challenge for Jayden. That's the only reason a man like him, one who had money, good looks and could easily have any woman he wanted, would pay someone so disconnected from the elite world they lived in a second glance.

But although she'd told herself time and time again that he'd eventually get bored and move on, the thought of losing him, of not enjoying his light-hearted and playful ways, it shook her to the point that she gripped the cushions of the sofa to steady herself.

Her brain continued to spiral out of control as she tried to anticipate his eventual letdown and somehow that fear turned to anger, taking control of her before she could stop her mouth from opening.

"So you're ending this?"

As he turned his face toward hers, she closed her eyes, not wanting to see rejection there.

"All my life, I've dealt with Sanford hating me

simply because I was too uncultured, too comfortable with 'slumming,' as he calls it. He's always hated me for my apparent affinity to what he sees as the ailments of poverty. I'm used to him rejecting me because I don't love the trappings of wealth the way he does. But I never thought you'd push me away for the same reason."

She felt him stiffen on the cushions next to her. Finally, she found the courage to open her eyes, determined not to let him see the hurt and disappointment cutting through her soul.

"What the hell did you just say to me?" Confused, she lifted a brow, sitting straighter on the sofa, trying to figure out where all this was leading. Rejection, she'd expected to see it. But there was bright rage that flamed so hot in the depths of his gaze, it shook her to her core.

"I'm done apologizing for not being the daughter he wants. I'm done with apologizing for not being born into wealth and for wanting to help people who are the most vulnerable among us because it somehow sullies rich people's need to enjoy everything their money can buy them. So if you're going to break up with me because I'll never fit into your world, just get it over with. I won't say I expected it, or even wanted it. But I for damn sure won't beg you to stay."

His jaw dropped as she glared at him. He seemed to be ready to say something, but he closed his mouth, taking a long, slow breath, as if he needed time to gather himself before responding to her.

"I was pissed because for the two minutes we spoke, he used one and a half to berate you. Standing there listening to the disrespectful filth he was spewing got under my skin."

The muscles in his face tightened until she could see his jaw flexing.

"But now I'm pissed for a whole different reason."

The fiery anger she was feeling gave way to icy fear. Had she misread things?

"Jayden—"

"Shut up." The words were quiet, yet so powerful she complied instantly. "Not another damn word until I'm finished."

Fire burned through him as he watched the vibrant, beautiful woman he'd come to care so much for accuse him of the vilest behavior.

"Zanai, how could you for even a moment think I shared any views Sanford could have about you? After all this time, how could you think I cared about something as trivial as you not being one of the spoiled brats born to the wealthy families of Royal?"

"Jayden, I didn't mean—"

"The hell you didn't." He barked those words at her. He wasn't prone to yelling, especially at women, his mother had raised him better than that. But the very idea that he could be so superficial and void of basic human decency pissed him the hell off.

"Zanai—" He stopped himself, whatever he was about to say leaving him as he met the confusion in her eyes. Her father had shaped her thoughts of rich people, had told her she didn't fit in and that something was wrong with her for wanting to be around people who didn't come from means. And now she was painting him with the same brush and he couldn't stand it.

"You know what? I'm going to show you better than I can tell you. Come with me." He grasped her hand, pulling her up from the sofa and leading her up the stairs to the standing mirror in his bedroom.

"What do you see?"

His voice was sharper than he intended. But he didn't apologize for it. He was too angry with Sanford for poisoning her mind against people like him, and he was angry with Zanai for buying into her father's bullshit.

It stopped tonight.

"Tell me what you see, Zanai."

"I see me."

He shook his head, folding his arms to keep his hands off her. As angry as he was right now, he couldn't trust himself not to try to shake some sense into her.

"No, you don't. You couldn't possibly see yourself, because if you did, you'd know there's nothing all the angels in heaven could tell me about you that would make me crave you any less. If you truly saw yourself as I see you, then you'd know the only thing Sanford made me believe today is that it would be thoroughly worth the risk of getting thrown in a holding cell at the sheriff's office just to have the satisfaction of popping that smug son of bitch in his mouth."

He unfolded his arms, stepping closer to her. Leaning down toward her ear as if he was whispering a precious secret to her.

"I'm so gone over you, Zanai, that I was ready to lay my hands on your father for disrespecting you in my presence. I'm so turned out that I had to war with myself about whether I would skip the emergency meeting my family had with the PI today or go to you and make sure you were safe and protected from Sanford's hate."

She visibly trembled, stoking his hunger for her, twisting it up with his anger to make it a dangerous mix of emotion and need that he was afraid he wouldn't be able to handle. But when he met her eyes through the mirror, and saw the same lust, the same need to consume and be consumed, he knew there wasn't a chance in hell of him walking away now.

"I fucking crave you, woman. Like air, like a vital nutrient my body needs to function. How dare you or anyone else try to diminish the dominion you wield so naturally over me? How dare you assume that my wealth and standing in this community is more important to me than you? I wouldn't care if you didn't fit into my world, which is the furthest thing from the truth, by the way. I'd turn my back on all of this bullshit in heartbeat just to be with you."

He let his thumb travel the supple line of her neck, loving the feeling of her racing pulse beneath her skin. He wrapped his opposite hand around her waist, pulling her against the hard wall of his body so she could feel him, feel what she did to him by simply being near him.

"I don't call you 'queen' because it's cute, Zanai." He unzipped the simple dress she wore and watched through the mirror as it slid off her body, exposing hard nipples through the lacy cups of her bra.

God, she was perfection. Standing there with her so close, he couldn't resist the need to slide his hand over her hip and finger the thin scrap of lace covering her mound. He fiddled with it until his fingers were beneath it, traveling down until they met the wet heat of her sex, drawing an audible moan from both of them when he slid so easily between her folds.

"I call you 'queen' because whether I'm in or out of your presence, the only thing I want to do is serve you, please you, protect you, worship you, sacrifice for you."

The circular rhythm of his fingers increased and her hips instinctively bucked, chasing the pleasure his touch gave her. "My devotion to you is proof that by divine right, you are majesty born. And if it's the last thing I do, I'm going to burn every negative lie Sanford James has ever made you believe about yourself and people like me until you understand that the only thing I could ever see you as is the powerful and compassionate woman that I can't get enough of."

She was riding his fingers now, her head fell back against his chest, her jaw hanging open as she moaned so beautifully for him. When she closed her eyes, he raised his free hand to her throat, applying slight pressure there as he spoke to her.

"Open your goddamn eyes. I want you to see what you do to me, what pleasing you does to me."

She obeyed and that fact made his dick so hard the jeans he was wearing were acting more like a tourniquet than clothing, cutting off much-needed blood flow. She was close, he could tell by the tremble of her thighs and the desperation in her wide eyes.

He moved his hand from her throat, filling it with one heavy breast, tweaking its nipple as she climbed higher, reaching for satisfaction.

"Do it," he whispered, his voice low and rough, scraping against his throat as the sound banged against the wall of his pharynx, through his mouth and finally floated on the air next to her ear. "Watch yourself come for me. See what I see every time you allow me to touch you like this. See how beautiful and powerful you are when you trust me enough to take care of you."

He scraped his teeth against the shell of her ear, tipping her over the edge. She screamed as she climaxed. The sound was animalistic, a roar that echoed across every wall and surface in his home, letting the world know she'd arrived, and was claiming everything, and everyone in her kingdom, because it was her right. And when she raised her arm, gripping her hand at the back of his neck, digging her nails into him, unafraid to mark him because he was hers to do with as she pleased, all he could think was *Thank you for finally realizing I'm yours.*

Fourteen

Jayden carried her to his bed, laying her down gently as if he was worried she would break.

That concern was understandable considering the way her body collapsed against his when she'd climaxed. She also understood that her track record of doubting him, and herself, probably made him uncertain of where her head was. She'd come to realize doubt was a joy killer. After standing in front of that mirror with him, so brazen and unencumbered with the weight of uncertainties, she decided she'd never miss another moment of happiness because she was too busy wallowing in the steady diet of doubt that Sanford had fed her for most of her life.

No more.

Whether Jayden stayed or not, watching herself come undone by his touch finally did make her see what Jayden had spent so much time trying to drill into her head. He wanted her. There wasn't any plan behind it, and he couldn't care less about what the rich and famous of Royal had to say about it. All he wanted…was her.

The confidence she'd displayed as she took everything she wanted from him broke the bonds of fear and doubt she'd struggled against for more years than she could count.

She was fearless as she stared at the wanton creature who had no hang-ups or misgivings about chasing the satisfaction she knew was within her grasp. It was hers to have, he was hers to have, and she would take as much pleasure and as much of him as she wanted.

Jayden quickly removed his clothing, positioning himself between her legs as he braced his weight on his arms.

"Every time I see you let your disbelief in me show, it's like a gut punch. I've done everything I can to show you what you mean to me, that I'm sincere. The fact that you still think I could be playing games with you, it's an insult, and quite frankly, it's really pissing me off. You're calling me a liar. I'm done allowing you to question my motives, my integrity. It's as simple as this—" his voice dropped down to its lower register, the deep baritone rumbling through her, breaking every chain of suspicion that lingered in the far reaches of her heart and mind "—I want you because you're everything, Zanai."

He spoke her name like a whispered prayer, reverent, sacred, necessary. It fueled her, emboldened her, making her reach for him, wrapping her arms around his broad chest and pulling him to her.

She draped her legs around him, using his surprise at her making such a bold move as an opportunity to roll them until she was straddling him.

She could understand the shock in his eyes. She'd held back for so long, only allowing glimpses of her true self to shine through for fear he'd reject her, or worse, criticize her and detail every way she didn't belong. But tonight, she could stop holding herself back.

The look of need burning in his eyes was the only permission she needed to do what she wanted. And right now, the only thing she wanted was to indulge in the delicacy that was Jayden Lattimore.

She started by capturing his mouth in hers. There was no hesitation, no preamble, only sheer lust. Her lips were insistent, demanding entry that he willingly gave her. His compliance was fuel to the blaze of need consuming her.

On a mission to satisfy the ache inside of her, she tore her mouth away from his, kissing down the sharp angle of his jaw, his neck and chest, licking and nipping his glorious, rich dark skin. She made her way down his torso, until she reached the coarse thatch of hair at his groin.

"Zanai, you don't—"

She didn't give him a chance to finish his sentence. She was determined to take what she wanted and the only thing she wanted was to consume the amazing man beneath her.

She eagerly continued, licking his length from root to tip, loving the full-body shudder, and the almost visceral "fuck" that escaped his lips. Satisfied he was just as into this as she was, she circled her tongue around the tip, gathering the pearl of his arousal, moaning her delight.

Too ravenous to linger, she wrapped her hand around the base of his cock, loving the feel of his girth in the palm of her hand as she slowly took him into her mouth, internally celebrating the long moan of satisfaction that escaped his lips.

Using her mouth and hand, she created an aching pattern of movement that had Jayden spreading his legs. At first, she thought it was just to give her more room to work, but soon, she realized it wasn't just for her comfort, but his need.

He planted one foot against the mattress, using it to gain purchase as his hips joined in the sensual rhythm she'd established.

She allowed him that boon, but refused to permit him to lead this dance. She wanted Jayden at her mercy the way she'd always been at his, and she refused to relinquish even the slightest bit of power now that she had him just where she wanted him.

She picked up the pace, one hand at the base of his cock, the other cradling his testicles with gentle pressure.

"Zanai." It was a warning mixed with a plea, and everything in her wanted to answer his need, to give them both what they so desperately desired.

She glanced up at him, taking in the beautiful image of the taut muscles of his body, of his face contorted by pleasure, realizing she'd never been so aroused or felt so powerful in her life. Without question, she knew this was where she belonged, with him, where every touch they shared was always welcomed and needed.

With one final twist of her hand she cupped her tongue against the underside of his cock. He laced strong fingers through her hair, as he thrust upward, calling out her name in sharp, broken syllables as he toppled over into bliss.

She swallowed his essence, licking him clean while humming softly against his flesh as his body relaxed beneath hers. She released him, kissing a path up his body, back to his mouth, loving how he pressed his lips against hers with such desperation, even after experiencing such a powerful release.

When they finally broke apart, there was something so intense swirling in the depths of his eyes, she nearly pulled away. He threaded his fingers into her hair, making sure she couldn't look away as he stared into her soul and said, "I love you."

She didn't have a chance to respond. He kissed her again, short-circuiting her brain, and eradicating any fears that tried to fill her skittish heart. And as he tucked her into his side, tightening his hold on her, she realized this was exactly where she needed to be. In his arms where nothing and no one in the outside world could touch her.

Daylight filtered through the curtains in his bedroom, dragging him from slumber. He stretched, smiling at the delightful ache of letting Zanai use his body in every way she wanted.

He was sure bruises and scratch marks would reveal themselves later, and he couldn't find a damn to give about it.

She'd taken everything she wanted. She didn't ask, she took, and it stoked his need so much, his dick was already rising with each sultry memory that danced across his closed lids.

He turned over, his hands instinctively reaching for warm flesh. When all he felt was cool bedding, he sat up searching the room for her.

The cottage was still, so much so, he instinctively knew he was alone. He quickly looked at the clock to see it was just past seven in the morning.

He ignored the disappointment growing in his

chest, reaching for his phone and finding a folded piece of paper from Zanai waiting for him.

Two words were displayed on the flap: *Thank you*.

There was a finality to those words that hollowed him out like an empty piece of deadwood drying up in the Texas heat.

Brittle was the only word that even came close to what he was feeling. He couldn't breathe, he couldn't move, every thought of losing her beating against him like a merciless body shot, breaking something vital inside him.

He lay back down, looking at the irony of the situation. He'd wanted her to be confident, to recognize her worth. And now that she had, she'd found the strength to leave him and his heart behind.

He didn't even try to deny it. He was in love with her. He'd said as much last night. His heart belonged to her, and thinking she might not want it had him lying in bed, staring up at his ceiling, wondering how he was going to deal with all of this if her note was the Dear John letter his mind told him it was. Deciding it was better to know the truth than speculate, he opened the note and read.

Zanai opened the door to the house she lived in with her father and his wife, slowly cataloguing everything around her.

There were no pictures of her up on the walls, no moments from her childhood displayed with pride.

It was as if she didn't truly exist in this place. The realization made her shiver. This wasn't her home. The people who lived here weren't her family.

She stepped farther into the house. Seeing the family room and the kitchen were empty, she headed toward Sanford's office located in one of the more remote sections of the house. She knocked on the door, not waiting for an answer before she opened it and stepped across the threshold. She didn't care what he was doing on the other side of the door, Sanford was going to make time to hear what she had to say.

"Well, look what the cat dragged in. Since I didn't see your car last night, I assume you spent the night with that Lattimore boy, didn't you?"

She didn't dignify his question with a response. She was an adult and she'd finally realized she didn't need to share anything about her life she didn't choose to and it didn't matter that the person doing the asking was her father.

"You were out of line accusing Jayden of trying to use me to get to you."

Sanford glanced up at her, offering a nonchalant snort. "Did you actually come here to defend your little lover? I do assume that's why you've found the courage to barge into my office giving me *tone*."

The word *tone* was bathed in derision. Before Jayden, she would've cowered under that dirty look her father was currently throwing at her. But today, she was her own woman and she wasn't going to allow him to throw dirt on her or Jayden.

"Telling you that you were out of line with the disrespectful accusations you lobbed at Jayden and me is not giving you tone. It's telling you that you were wrong."

"I was wrong?" Both brows stretched toward his hairline as his question floated in the air. "I'll give that young man credit. He's actually got you believing you're more than the mealymouthed waste of time you've always been."

The words should've hurt a lot more than they did. But sadly, for him anyway, she wasn't the same little girl seeking her father's approval. As an adult, she now realized she'd never have it.

She huffed, mourning all the years she'd wasted because she hadn't yet come to that realization.

"Stay away from Jayden. My relationship with him is none of your concern."

"You walk into my house telling me what I will and won't do? Little girl, you forget yourself. You are nothing but what I allow you to be. And my benevolence is reaching its breaking point."

Rage, raw and blinding, colored her sight. This man, her own father, believed she was his to command.

"If you'd clear your head of all that boy's charm, you'd realize I'm actually trying to protect you. We both know you're not in that man's league. What other reason could he have to be with you other than to get to me?"

She dropped her gaze to the floor, not because she was afraid to look at Sanford, not even because she was hurt by his cruel words. Again, regret filled her as she thought about how much time she'd lost caring what this man thought of her.

"Would it kill you to support my decisions and show at least a small modicum of faith in me?"

"Would it kill you to give me a reason to?"

The nerve of this man was galling. Why she was surprised, she didn't know. Sanford had never shown her any kindnesses.

"Why do you hate me? What have I ever done to make you not love me?"

He casually laced his fingers together as if they were having a mundane chat that held no consequences.

"You're weak, Zanai. And I despise weakness. I've tried my best to rid you of it and nothing has worked. I've given you everything, and all you've done is thrown it back in my face. You're too much like your mother, you still can't seem to find your backbone. And just like her, the world is going to chew you up and spit you out because you're so broken. Mark my words, it won't be long before you're taking the easy way out just like she did."

The mention of her mother in such a context made rage rush through her bloodstream.

"You drove my mother to killing herself and then profited off her death. Don't you ever speak of her like that again. You are a heartless creature that never deserved the beauty and grace she embodied. My only consolation is that life will deal with you much better than I can. When it does, you'd best believe I'm gonna pull up a chair, kick my heels up and chomp on popcorn as I watch everything you value burn to cinders."

It might've been a tad dramatic, but she'd meant every word of that tirade. She didn't know how or when, but he would get his comeuppance, the universe always balanced itself out. Knowing how her mother had suffered through their toxic relationship, there had to be a hell in which Sanford James was going to burn.

"Impressive." He nodded as he readjusted himself in his seat. "But I'm done. I demand better from you. On this I will not budge. You will end whatever this thing is you share with Lattimore and that's it. He's either trying to mess with my business, or worse, he and his kind are looking to make me look bad through you. Either way, I've worked too hard to let the Lattimores and their ilk take anything from me."

"He's a rancher for God's sake. What could he possibly want with your business?"

He shrugged. "Don't know. Don't care. But there's no way someone like him comes down off his perch to wallow in the gutter unless it will benefit him."

His self-centered paranoia made absolutely no sense. She realized trying to dig any deeper wouldn't yield any different results, so she tilted her head and asked, "Is that your final word?"

She widened her stance and braced herself as if she were expecting a blow. Sanford had never laid a hand on her throughout her life. That didn't mean that he hadn't left lasting marks on her soul.

"That is my final word."

"Well," she huffed, "that's too bad. Because there's no way in hell I'm letting the best thing that's ever happened to me go. Especially for some imagined threat your ego has cooked up. Contrary to what you believe, you are not a rival to the Lattimores. Not just in your net worth, but in your composition as a human being. You've got nothing on those folks. You've got nothing on me. And I refuse to listen to your garbage for one more minute."

A wry grin spread across his face until it morphed into the malicious laughter that was meant to do nothing but intimidate her.

"Zanai, I've used up as much grace as I care to on you. I'm done. This is my house; you are my daughter and you will obey me. Otherwise, you can leave my key on my desk and get the hell out."

She looked into his soulless eyes and realized he meant every word he'd spoken. The thought of homelessness should've frightened her, should've made her give in. She was employed, so of course she could carry the financial weight of being on her own. What should've been daunting was facing the world on her own terms. But as she saw the pleasure he took in bullying her, she realized there were worse fates than being kicked out of Sanford's house. The one in particular that came to mind was the threat of losing herself forever if she remained under his thumb.

She couldn't do it. She couldn't spend one more moment doubting herself and being tortured by the so-called family who was supposed to love her.

Without speaking another word, she removed the house keys from the metal ring securing them, and turned toward the door.

"Don't come back. Don't even think about taking anything in your room either. If it's in my house, it's mine. See what it is to truly fend for yourself."

Again, she didn't say a word, she simply opened the door and stepped through it and into her future. Now, all she had to do was convince Jayden to be part of that future and everything would be fine.

And as she stepped out of the house, smiling at the warm Texas sun sitting high in the sky, she realized that as much as it would hurt, as much as the thought of losing Jayden felt as if she would lose something precious to her physical being, she knew if it came to that, she would live. She was strong enough to face whatever came her way. And for the things she couldn't handle, she was fortunate enough to have access to the tools that would help her deal with them.

This was her path, and she would gladly walk it.

Fifteen

Jayden sat at his table holding the folded piece of paper between his fingers like it was a ticking bomb. Every time he opened it, rereading it over and over again to make sure he'd read it correctly, he felt like a timer was ticking away with each beat of his heart.

Dear Jayden,
Thank you for showing me who I am. Sorry to leave without saying goodbye, but there's something I have to do, something I've been putting off too long. It was the coward's way of running away like a thief in the night, but if I'd woken to see your powerful gaze, or your

warm smile, there would be no way I could willingly separate myself from that even for a brief few moments.

He sat there, with the letter in one hand and his phone in the other, looking back and forth between the two. He was stuck, he wanted to call and demand answers, but deep down he knew if he heard her voice, he'd be reduced to begging her to come back. And he couldn't do that.

He would not do that.

Sure, he wanted her. No, that wasn't right—he needed her. He needed her in his arms the way his brain needed oxygen and his lungs craved air. But if he asked her to return, he'd never know if it was because she wanted to be by his side, or if she was simply doing it because he wanted her to.

After everything, after every moment of pleasure they'd wrung from each other's bodies, after baring his soul to her in every way he knew how, she'd still left. The only recourse for him now was to respect her decision and let her be. Otherwise, he'd be no better than her father who'd tried to control her by withholding love and diminishing her fire, and manipulating her into believing she wasn't worthy of his love.

He would never do that to her. With that decision firmly made, the only thing his aching heart could do was continue to leak his love and joy until his insides were a bloody, inoperable mess.

He thought about how broken he was in this moment, and his face contorted into a derisive sneer. He'd told himself and Zanai this was just for fun. Developing feelings for her beyond the desire he instinctively experienced every time she was near was not in his plan. But somehow, he landed in this space where his entire world stopped spinning because she'd walked away.

In the distance, he heard a knock on his front door, but couldn't find the strength to get up and answer it. Whoever it was on the other side of it, he knew he didn't want to see them. He wasn't fit for company, especially not from one of his family members who would take one look at him and know something was wrong.

How could he explain that he, the master of relaxed and unbothered, was so tied up in knots over a woman that every breath felt like a laborious undertaking?

The knocking didn't cease, irritating his already foul mood. He pushed himself to his feet, taking hard steps toward the door, making the room around him vibrate from the force of his gait.

"Jonathan, if that's you, I'm taking the day off."

His brother didn't answer, so Jayden yanked the door open, nearly losing his balance when he saw who was on the other side.

"Jayden, are you okay?"

The sight of Zanai was water to a man wandering the desert aimlessly. He extended his hand, wanting to see if she was real or if this was a cruel mirage his battered heart had created, but stopped midway between them.

"What are you doing here?"

She braced against the question. Her knitted brows drew tightly together as she gazed at him.

"Didn't you get my note?"

"Oh." He spoke on a weak laugh that was filled with snark. "I got your note all right."

He stepped away from the door, leaving it open for her to walk in if she wanted. Even now, when he ached with this strange mix of anger and need, he couldn't find the strength to turn her away.

He flopped down on his couch, stretching out lengthwise so she'd have to sit on one of the armchairs. The scent of her was already far too enticing, having her near enough to touch was too much for him to handle.

"According to your note, you were leaving. What are you doing back here? I thought you were gone."

God, he could taste the acrid bitterness on his tongue with each word spoken. She'd changed him on a chemical level, and now his brain was stuck on stupid with disappointment and pain, leaving him unable to temper his speech and keep the emotion out of his words.

"To go take care of something," she responded, pulling his gaze toward hers. There was something about the way she said those words that gave him pause, like he was missing something important in the delivery of the message.

"But your note said you left."

"Temporarily, yes. I needed to see Sanford this morning and set some things straight before I could come back here. I was kind of hoping you'd still be asleep and I could slip right back into bed with you without you noticing. Except I didn't realize the slam lock was on and I didn't have a key to get back in, hence the loud knocking."

He sat up, locking gazes with her as he processed what she'd said. "You intended to come back?"

He could see the moment that something clicked in her head, as if she was finally understanding his words. She stood, taking slow steps to cross the small distance from her armchair, to the sofa he was sitting on.

When she reached him, she kneeled down between his legs, placing her hands on his thighs.

"You thought I wasn't coming back?" It was phrased as a question, but the stern glint in her eye made it a statement. She was declaring this, no doubt about it.

"Jayden, you've spent the majority of our relationship reassuring me. Let me return the favor. There is nothing and no one who will ever make me walk away from you. Not anymore."

He could feel the muscles in his jaw tightening. The mere thought of there being anyone who could separate them made his anger rise.

There wasn't anyone else. He knew that. The way her body craved his, the way she responded to his touch, there was no way she was involved with anyone else romantically. He'd stake his life on that.

But they both knew Zanai was skittish, always ready to turn and run from the things burning between them. Hell, she wasn't just ready to run, she'd actually done so. It was only through serendipity that he'd discovered the identity of his disappeared red queen.

"After last night, something changed for me, Jayden. It wasn't just about great sex. Something clicked into place the way it never has before."

She rubbed her hands up and down the ridges of his thighs. It was an absentminded gesture, but to him, the feel of her when she was so near stoked an almost Pavlovian response, him wanting to feel her bare flesh against him.

"I've spent so much time focusing on the problems of others as a means to avoid dealing with my own issues. As much as I love my job and the good it does, it's become a shield against the wounds I've spent a lifetime trying to cover up."

He opened his mouth to speak, but she held up a hand, silencing him.

"Please," she begged. "Let me get this out while

I still can." He gave her a curt nod in response and she continued.

"The doubting you and myself to boot, it was all there because I feared turning into my mother. That fear was the reason Sanford has been able to make me forget who I could be."

She inched the fingers of one hand up until they were touching his, lacing them together in a beautiful latticework.

"From the moment I met you, you've poured your belief into me, and it's finally paid off because when you told me Sanford had cornered you, I was no longer afraid. Instead, I was mad. Mad enough, I needed to give him a piece of my mind. The only reason I was so angry was I knew Sanford was trying to take something away from me, something that was mine, something I deserved."

"Zanai," he huffed, his countenance wearing thinner every time her doubt in him surfaced. "I would never allow anyone to tell me who you are. Not after spending time with you, not after touching you. I knew everything I needed to know about you the moment we met. I wanted you, and if that were so, it was only because you were worthy of my desire."

A slow smile spread across her face, softening her features, making him want to pull her to him, and press his lips against hers.

"I know that now. I really know that. Because when I woke up this morning, I had to go see Sanford and let him know he couldn't turn you against me. That you'd never leave because of something he said. That I would never let you go at his command."

Those words unlocked the cage imprisoning his beating heart. The constriction of anger and fear fell away, leaving it room to pump as fast and strong as his love burned for her.

"I can't imagine he took that well." Jayden only knew Sanford by reputation and their brief exchange on the street. Neither scenario particularly warmed Jayden enough to the man to want to spend time getting to know what made him tick. But even still, the fact that Sanford was a bully, especially when it came to his own daughter, was unmistakable.

"He didn't. He huffed and puffed and when that didn't work, he threatened."

Jayden tensed, the idea of Sanford, or anyone else for that matter, bringing harm to her made every muscle he had stiffen in preparation for a fight.

But she raised a hand to his cheek, gently rubbing her thumb against the skin there, slowly stroking his anger away.

"He threatened me. But when he saw his threats fell on deaf ears, he stooped to the only tactic he had left in his arsenal. He threw me out."

Jayden closed his eyes and took a slow, deep breath, trying his best to keep his anger in check. Anger clouded his mind, and he desperately needed a clear head to listen to what Zanai had to tell him.

"Did you bring your belongings with you? If so, I've got plenty of storage space."

"That's sweet of you to offer." She leaned in giving him a brief kiss. It was so soft and fleeting he could hardly believe it happened, the resulting flame being the only proof of her touch. "But he wouldn't let me leave with anything."

"Your things, Zanai—"

"—are just things, Jayden." Her smile was so bright and charming, he couldn't see any pain or apprehension there. Whatever had transpired between Zanai and her father, it didn't seem to bring on the distress just the mere mention of his name created the night before.

"I've always known Sanford would get tired of me underfoot, sooner or later. Living rent free all this time has allowed me to put enough money away that I should be fine getting a place of my own. All of the really important things like my mother's jewelry and mementos, my identification, and my degrees and licensure, I moved into a safe-deposit box a long time ago. The only thing left in that house were clothes, and things that can be easily replaced. And since my bestie owns a clothing boutique, finding new clothes won't be a problem."

He went to speak, but she placed a delicate finger over his mouth, silencing him before the words could slip into the air.

"You don't have to worry about me, Jayden. That

frail woman who was afraid to live her life outside
of the confines of the prison Sanford locked her in,
she's gone. I can do this."

There was determination in her eyes like he'd
never seen before. A strength that always seemed
to simmer just below the surface, but now, was on
full display, intoxicating his senses.

"I've already contacted a Realtor. I'll start looking at some listings tomorrow. I just need a place to
stay tonight. Would you be willing to let me crash
on your couch?"

He quickly pulled her up from her kneeling position on the floor, settling her on his lap, then clasping
his hand around the back of her neck, drawing her to
him. Before she could say another word, his lips were
against hers in a fierce kiss that sent him reeling.

This woman. This smart, sexy and infinitely capable woman had finally stepped into her own and
he'd never found her sexier as a result.

"Cancel it."

She pulled back, her dark questioning gaze falling onto his face.

"Cancel what?"

"Your appointment with the Realtor. Stay here."

The "with me" part disintegrated on his tongue
the moment he pulled her down for another kiss. She
was free now. Finally free to fully step into her own,
and he didn't want to miss one second of it.

"You mean, indefinitely?"

"I mean, as in move in with me."

"I couldn't impo—"

He kissed her again, stopping whatever nonsense she was about to speak into the air.

"I love you, Zanai. More than I thought I ever could. I want you with me all the time. If that's not what you want or if you don't feel the same way, I'll certainly understand. But I need you to know my intentions are to be with you and only you. Just give me the chance and I'll prove to you how much you mean to me."

She pulled his hand from her neck, burrowing her cheek into it as she moaned his name. And the sound of it, the way every syllable slipped from her full, soft lips had his cock aching to slide into her.

And he would.

He had all intentions of burying himself to the hilt inside the tightness of her warmth. But first things first, he needed to convince her this was where she belonged, by his side.

"You've already proven it to me, Jayden. Now it's time for me to prove myself to you."

She stared intently at him, as if to make sure she had all his attention. She needn't have worried about that. His attention was always on her.

"I love you, Jayden."

Those four words spoken so softly he could hardly believe they'd escaped her mouth, cracked his chest open leaving his heart vulnerable and exposed. Fear should be welling up inside him as a result. Instead, a calm assurance fell over him, letting him know everything would be all right.

"I want nothing more than to spend the rest of my life with you."

"That sounded vaguely like a proposal."

She giggled softly. "To shack up, not get married. At least not yet. Let's see how this living together thing works before we cross that particular bridge."

The languid sensation of happiness flowing through him curved his lips into a playful smile. "Then you'll give me pretty words and my ring."

"Then—" she paused, leaning down to kiss him, slipping her tongue into his willing mouth "—then, I will give you anything you want, for as long as you want it."

"Well, since you won't give me my ring right now, maybe you'll at least accept a small token from me. Sort of a pre-engagement gift, if there is such a thing."

He leaned over to open the coffee-table drawer, pulling out the red jewelry box.

He handed it to her, and her face lit up with anticipation. She carefully opened it and her eyes glazed over in awe of what she found inside.

"Jayden, when did you…? Why…?"

He took the opened box from her, removing the necklace from its cushioned bed, and carefully placed it around her neck as she held her hair up for him.

"After you fit in so well with my family at the cookout, I knew I wanted you near me as often as possible. And I wanted to be near you. So I gave the jeweler a picture of the earring you left behind and had him create a companion piece for your neck. I wanted it to be a necklace because I wanted to give you something that would remind you of me and how we met, and have it lay close to your heart."

Tears slid down her face as a wobbly smile curved her lips.

"This is stunning," she whispered. "I love it, and I love you."

His heart stuttered in his chest, stealing his breath and his ability to speak. This woman had changed him, made him reach for something other than "a good time." She'd burrowed underneath his skin and permanently nested her love inside of him, effectively taking control of his being.

That should've terrified him. It should've made him run for the proverbial hills. Instead, the only thing he wanted was to draw her closer and never let her go. His red queen had finally arrived to reign over his heart and he couldn't be happier.

"That, Dr. James—" he punctuated his words with soft kisses along the curve of her neck, drawing the pretty sounds he ached to hear from her "—is exactly what I wanted to hear."

* * * * *

Don't miss the next book in the
Texas Cattleman's Club: Ranchers and Rivals
One Christmas Night
by Jules Bennett

WE HOPE YOU ENJOYED
THIS BOOK FROM

HARLEQUIN
DESIRE

*Luxury, scandal, desire—welcome to
the lives of the American elite.*

Be transported to the worlds of oil barons, family dynasties, moguls and celebrities. Get ready for juicy plot twists, delicious sensuality and intriguing scandal.

6 NEW BOOKS AVAILABLE EVERY MONTH!

#2911 ONE CHRISTMAS NIGHT
Texas Cattleman's Club: Ranchers and Rivals
by Jules Bennett
Ryan Carter and Morgan Grandin usually fight like cats and dogs—until one fateful night at a Texas Cattleman's Club masquerade ball. Now will an unexpected pregnancy make these hot-and-heavy enemies permanent lovers?

#2912 MOST ELIGIBLE COWBOY
Devil's Bluffs • by Stacey Kennedy
Brokenhearted journalist Adeline Harlow is supposed to write an exposé on Colter Ward, Texas's Sexiest Bachelor, *not* fall into bed with him enthusiastically and repeatedly! If only it's enough to break their no-love-allowed rule for a second chance at happiness...

#2913 A VALENTINE FOR CHRISTMAS
Valentine Vineyards • by Reese Ryan
Prodigal son Julian Brandon begrudgingly returns home to fulfill a promise. Making peace with his troubled past and falling for sophisticated older woman Chandra Valentine aren't part of the plan. But what is it they say about best-laid plans...?

#2914 WORK-LOVE BALANCE
Blackwells of New York • by Nicki Night
When gorgeous TV producer Jordan Chambers offers Ivy Blackwell the chance of a lifetime, the celebrated heiress and social media influencer wonders if she can handle his tempting offer...and the passion that sizzles between them!

#2915 TWO RIVALS, ONE BED
The Eddington Heirs • by Zuri Day
Stakes can't get much higher for attorneys Maeve Eddington and Victor Cortez in the courtroom...or in the bedroom. With family fortunes on the line, these rivals will go to any lengths to win. But what if love is the ultimate prize?

#2916 BILLIONAIRE MAKEOVER
The Image Project • by Katherine Garbera
When PR whiz Olive Hayes transforms scruff CEO Dante Russo into the industry's sexiest bachelor, she realizes she's equally vulnerable to his charms. But is she falling for her new creation or the man underneath the makeover?

SPECIAL EXCERPT FROM

Ⓗ HARLEQUIN

DESIRE

*Thanks to violinist Megan Han's one-night fling with her
father's new CFO, Daniel Pak, she's pregnant! No one
can know the truth—especially not her matchmaking
dad, who'd demand marriage. If only her commitment-
phobic not-so-ex lover would open his heart...*

Read on for a sneak peek at
One Night Only
by Jayci Lee.

The sway of Megan's hips mesmerized him as she glided
down the walkway ahead of him. He caught up with her
in three long strides and placed his hand on her lower
back. His nostrils flared as he caught a whiff of her sweet
floral scent, and reason slipped out of his mind.

He had been determined to keep his distance since
the night she came over to his place. He didn't want to
betray Mr. Han's trust further. And it wouldn't be easy
for Megan to keep another secret from her father. The
last thing he wanted was to add to her already full plate.
But when he saw her standing in the garden tonight—a
vision in her flowing red dress—he knew he would crawl
through burning coal to have her again.

She reached for his hand, and he threaded his fingers through hers, and she pulled them into a shadowy alcove and pressed her back against the wall. He placed his hands on either side of her head and stared at her face until his eyes adjusted to the dark. He sucked in a sharp breath when she slid her palms over his chest and wrapped her arms around his neck.

"I don't want to burden you with another secret to keep from your father." He held himself in check even as desire pumped through his veins.

"I think fighting this attraction between us is the bigger burden," she whispered. His head dipped toward her of its own volition, and she wet her lips. "What are you doing, Daniel?"

"Surviving," he said, his voice a low growl. "Because I can't live through another night without having you."

She smiled then—a sensual, triumphant smile—and he was lost.

Don't miss what happens next in...
One Night Only
by Jayci Lee.

Available December 2022 wherever
Harlequin Desire books and ebooks are sold.

Harlequin.com

Get 4 FREE REWARDS!

We'll send you 2 FREE Books plus 2 FREE Mystery Gifts.

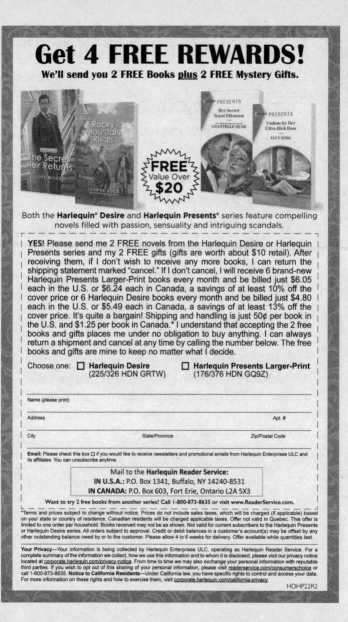

FREE Value Over **$20**

Both the **Harlequin® Desire** and **Harlequin Presents®** series feature compelling novels filled with passion, sensuality and intriguing scandals.

Love Harlequin romance?

DISCOVER.

Be the first to find out about promotions, news and exclusive content!

f Facebook.com/HarlequinBooks

🐦 Twitter.com/HarlequinBooks

📷 Instagram.com/HarlequinBooks

P Pinterest.com/HarlequinBooks

You Tube YouTube.com/HarlequinBooks

ReaderService.com

EXPLORE.

Sign up for the Harlequin e-newsletter and download a free book from any series at **TryHarlequin.com**

CONNECT.

Join our Harlequin community to share your thoughts and connect with other romance readers!
Facebook.com/groups/HarlequinConnection